The Chronicles of Paul

A Nurse Alissa Spin-off

The Chronicles of Paul

A Nurse Alissa Spin-off

Scott M. Baker

Also by Scott M. Baker

A Schattenseite Book

The Chronicles of Paul
A Nurse Alissa Spin-off
by Scott M. Baker.
Copyright © 2021. All Rights Reserved.
Print Edition
ISBN-13: 978-1-7365915-2-9

Cover Art © Christian Bentulan

Chapter One

"**W**HAT THE FUCK is taking so long," Paul Madison mumbled to himself.

He had been stuck in traffic along the Penn-Lincoln Parkway for over thirty minutes and had barely moved two car lengths. At first, he had blamed the tie up on the construction crew that had blocked the left lane for the past mile until he noticed that the road work ended well before the bridge.

Just as frustrating, he sat only two hundred feet from the onramp to Fort Pitt Bridge that would take him across the river and to the airport. He should have been there ten minutes ago to catch his flight to Logan Airport in Boston. He needed that time because dealing with TSA was always a time-consuming pain in the ass.

Opening the driver's door, Paul stood on the rental car's running board and checked out the situation ahead of him. Grid lock jammed both the upper and lower decks of the bridge. No one would be going anywhere for a while. Fuck it.

Climbing back inside, Paul switched the radio from Sirius to the local stations, hoping to catch a traffic update. He pulled his cellphone out of his shirt pocket to call ahead and change his flight time, pausing when the voice of the radio announcer came through the speakers.

…continue to come in from Pittsburgh and the surrounding suburbs. We have reports of people going mad and eating other people.… Bob, are you certain about this? Eating people?

Paul stared at the radio, aghast. Years ago, that drug addict in Florida had chewed off the face a homeless guy, but that had been an isolated incident. This was either typical media hype or some heavy-ass shit was going down. And he sat stalled in traffic at ground zero.

The reports of people eating their victims have been confirmed. One report indicates that a police unit attempting to quell a disturbance on Wylie Avenue was overrun and killed by rioters. Wait a minute. A pause elapsed. *I've just received a report informing me that the governor has declared a state of emergency for the Pitts—*

A monotone blare came across the speakers signifying the Emergency Broadcast System had clicked in. A moment later, the alert stopped.

This is the Emergency Broadcast System. This is not a test. I repeat, this is not a test. Uncontrolled violence has broken out in Philadelphia, Pittsburgh, Scranton, and other cities and towns throughout Pennsylvania. The governor has declared a State of Emergency effective immediately. Stay home and lock your doors, and do not let anyone inside. Those not at home should shelter in place until further notice. If you're out on the road or walking the streets, find a safe place to stay immediately. A twenty-four-hour curfew will go into effect in thirty minutes. Anyone caught outside after that time will be subject to detention. The Governor has mobilized the National Guard to deal with the rioters. The use of lethal force against anyone committing violence has been authorized. I repeat, the use of lethal force against anyone committing violence has been authorized.

God damn, thought Paul. This isn't a typical protest, not if the police can use lethal force. He was in the middle of a complete breakdown of the social order.

The yelling of a group of five road workers off to his left caught Paul's attention. He followed their gaze to a 737 that had taken off from the airport a few miles away. Rather than gain altitude, it made a sharp turn to make an emergency landing back on the runway. The aircraft skimmed the buildings in the suburbs west of the Monongahela River and turned over the waterway. It passed by the parkway, the tip of its right wing missing a crane by mere feet.

The 737 suddenly banked at a forty-five-degree angle. The left wing sliced through the river, throwing the aircraft into a somersault. The fuselage slammed into the river, breaking apart on impact. The right wing crashed into the center span of the Fort Pitt Bridge, ripping a fifteen-foot gap through the steel and concrete. Its fuel tanks exploded, instantly incinerating the vehicles on both levels closest to the site. Burning aviation fuel flowed along the road, igniting more vehicles, or poured into the river, creating flaming pools around the wreck. It would be a miracle if anyone from the plane survived.

One of the construction workers leaned against the crane and vomited. Paul didn't blame him. He had seen enough accidents and been in his fair share of bad incidents in the past, but nothing like this. This was a fucking nightmare. How could it get any worse?

Paul regretted asking that question when yelling came from the cars in front of him.

Chapter Two

NINE PEDESTRIANS WANDERED up from the lower level of Fort Pitt Bridge, survivors of the carnage. They must have been near the crash site because blood covered each of them. One victim in a Pittsburgh Police uniform had both arms torn off. The stomach of another, a young lady in a skirt and heels, had been gashed open. She raced up the ramp with her entrails dragging behind her. Stragglers stopped at the cars nearest the lower level, scratching at the windows trying to get at the drivers.

Five cars down, a middle-aged man with gray hair stepped out of his Mercedes and approached the wounded.

"I'm a doctor. Let me have a look—"

The victims lunged. Two each grabbed an arm and shoved the doctor against the Mercedes, then sank their teeth into his flesh. He screamed. Three more attacked, two going for each leg. The gutted female dropped in front of the doctor, tore open his shirt, and dug her fingers through his skin and into his abdomen, pulling out his intestines. The eighth victim and the armless police officer dropped to their knees and fed off the entrails.

An eerie pause fell over the parkway as the reality of the situation set in. These things were devouring the doctor. Only one possibility came to Paul's mind, though at first, he refused to believe it. He had prepared for every eventuality imaginable but never seriously considered this scenario. The dead had come back to live.

The road workers to his left reacted first, rushing into the fray to help the doctor. As they yanked away the living dead, the latter turned on the road workers, knocking them to the ground and feeding off them. A burly guy with red hair and a beard grabbed one of the living dead by the head and twisted, snapping its neck. Rather than drop to the ground, the thing remained standing, its head hanging to one side and facing to its rear. It shoved the red-headed worker to the ground where two more of the living dead crawled over to feed.

In the Audi Q3 directly behind the Mercedes, a young mother screamed as she watched the doctor being torn apart. Jumping out of the front seat, she ran around to the rear passenger door and pulled it open, reaching inside to remove her baby from the car seat. She might have snuck away if she had not been screaming at the top of her lungs. The commotion attracted five of the original living dead that jumped up from the ravaged doctor and hunted down the fresh kill. Three tackled the mother, dragging her to the pavement where they ripped off chunks of her flesh. Oblivious to her own suffering, the young woman struggled to get back up and rescue her child. It was far too late for that. The other two living dead crawled into the rear seat and attacked the howling infant, tearing off limbs and feeding as if it had been a roast chicken.

Paul checked his rearview mirror. No one had gotten out of their vehicles, still stunned by what they had witnessed. They would be dead in minutes. Exiting his rental car, Paul jumped onto the trunk and waved his hands.

"You're all in danger. Run while you have a chance."

A couple in the Toyota RAM behind him reacted first. Climbing out of the SUV, they took off down the parkway. Others quickly joined in. Within seconds, those trying to escape packed the road. At least they had a fighting chance.

A snarl came from behind him. One of the original nine deaders, a man in a gore-stained business suit, had heard Paul warning the others and rushed toward him. Paul jumped off the trunk and vaulted over the jersey barriers, then searched for a weapon. The closest was a hand-held grinder used to cut through concrete. He picked it up and switched it on. The circular blades sprang to life.

The deader in the business suit bounded over the barriers and charged, its mouth agape and its hands clutching for its food. When it drew closer, Paul raised the grinder and shoved it into the thing's face. The blade cut through the skull, cleaving it in half and generating a spray of blood and gore that splattered him. The living dead dropped to the road, motion-less.

A thud sounded beside him. The armless police officer had stumbled over the barrier and face planted itself onto the cement. It squirmed, trying to get up. Paul ran the grinder across its neck, severing the head. Paul placed the grinder on the ground and removed the officer's belt with his sidearm, spare ammo, and police radio. Once he secured the belt around his waist, Paul lifted the grinder and assessed the situation.

The female deader had tried to crawl over the barrier, getting its intestines caught in the rebar extending from the top. It yanked to get at him and would soon break free. The pack that had attacked the mother were still feeding. Another pack of deaders emerged from the lower level, checking each vehicle for food. The doctor and road workers climbed to their feet, reanimated and searching for food. No way he could take them all on. His old man used to say that discretion was the better part of valor. Paul ran, still carrying the grinder.

Two of the road workers and the doctor spotted him, jumped over the barrier, and gave chase. They closed the distance rapidly.

Paul spotted a front-loader one hundred feet ahead of him. In front of it sat a three-foot-square opening carved out of the parkway. It gave him an idea. He positioned himself between the front loader and the opening and waited, holding the grinder that whirred at full speed.

The doctor reached him first and charged. As Paul had hoped, it fell through the opening, shattering its head on the edge in front of Paul before plummeting to the ground beneath. One of the road workers jumped the gap. Paul ducked to one side. It slammed into the bucket of the front-loader and staggered back. Paul drove the grinder into its half-eaten face. The deader stumbled and dropped through the opening.

The second road worker circled around, rushing at Paul between the hole and the front-loader. Paul raised the grinder and shoved it into its chest. The blades ripped their way through its sternum and shredded its lungs and heart. The road worker thrashed about and reached out for Paul, knocking them both off balance. They tumbled toward the opening. Paul released his grip on the grinder and shoved it into the deader, pushing himself away in the process. The road worker toppled over and fell through the opening. Paul landed on his back, wincing from the pain that shot through his right shoulder blade. He twisted his arm. Thankfully, he did not break any bones, only bruised it. He could deal with that later. Right now, he needed to survive.

Another set of snarls attracted his attention. The last three road workers ran toward him. Paul scanned the area and spotted a three-foot-long crowbar lying on the ground two yards from him. He rolled over to it, the pain in his shoulder spiking. Grabbing the crowbar in his right hand, he jumped to his feet as the first road worker approached. Its shirt had been torn open and half its chest eaten. Paul swung the crowbar like a baseball bat, the hooked end colliding with the living dead's head. The road worker spun around and fell against the guard rail, spasming.

The second roadworker was only a few feet away. Its lower jaw had been torn off and its neck eaten, exposing the larynx. Paul spun the crowbar in his hands and drove the end into its neck, shattering the spine. The road worker fell to the cement, its body motionless but its head still snarling.

The third road worker lunged. Paul dropped to his hands and knees. The worker tripped over him, falling face first onto the road. Its skull fractured on impact, sending a spray of blood and teeth in all directions. Paul jumped up and drove the end of the crowbar into the back of its head, rupturing the top portion of its skull. Brains oozed out onto the cement. It still thrashed around, so Paul struck it again, this time in the lower half of its head. The metal went through, clinking on the cement. The road worker went limp.

Paul hid behind the front-loader to survey the situation. No more of the living dead were coming for him, which was a plus. On the downside, those remaining made their way down the line of parked cars, feeding off the few drivers and passengers who stayed with their vehicles, hoping they would be safe, a bad decision that had cost them their lives. More of the living dead moved along the eastbound side of the Pitt-Lincoln Parkway coming from the upper approaches of the Fort Pitt Bridge. If he moved now, he still had a chance of escaping.

Paul crossed over to the jersey barrier and, crouching so they wouldn't see him, ran down the parkway. He paused only once, just long enough to pick up a twenty-six-inch-long axe mattock resting against the barrier.

As Paul made his escape, he prayed none of the living dead were coming from the direction he was heading.

Chapter Three

PAUL PAUSED WHEN he reached the on/off ramp connecting the parkway to Fort Pitt Boulevard. He contemplated getting off here and abandoning the parkway, which severely limited his options, but decided against it. From this vantage point, he saw even more violence occurring in the streets of Pittsburgh. Thick, black smoke rose from several areas throughout the city. He stood a better chance on the parkway. Besides, he needed to cross the river over to the southern side where there were fewer people and more ways to escape. A bridge a quarter of a mile ahead of him offered the best chance.

Staying low, Paul made his way down the parkway.

Ten cars before reaching the bridge, he came across a Prius with a young woman still inside. At first, he thought she might be one of the living dead, only there was no blood inside the car and the occupant had her head on the steering wheel, crying. Every ounce of common sense, everything he had learned as a prepper, told him that stopping to help her would get him killed. Yet his humanity kicked in.

Paul crossed over the jersey barriers and knocked on the driver's side window.

The young woman sat up straight and leaned away from him. "Don't eat me. Leave me alone."

"Quiet," warned Paul. "Do you want to attract attention to us?"

"You're not of them?"

"Who?"

"The radio is calling them deaders, people who come back to life and eat the living. There's thousands of them in the city."

"I'm here to help you." Paul opened the door. The stupid bitch never thought to lock it. "Come with me if you want to live,"

Shit, thought Paul. *Can you get any more cliché?*

The young woman started to get out. She might not be the brightest bulb on the string of lights, but she was the prettiest. She wore jeans, dress boots, and an orange sweater that tightly fit her well-endowed chest. Her brunette hair was cut in a stylish bob. Even the large, circular glasses she wore did not distract from her good appearance.

She screamed, accompanied by a snarl to Paul's left. The mother killed trying to save her doctor raced toward them.

He placed the crowbar against the Prius and waited until it got close than whipped open the driver's door, slamming it into the deader's chest and stunning it. Taking the axe end of the mattock, Paul raised it and brought the blade down, smashing it into the top of the mother's skull. It pulled back, yanking itself off the blade, and fell against the jersey barrier, spasming.

A dozen more were only yards behind it.

Paul yanked the young woman out of the Prius and slid into the driver's seat. Shifting into gear, he pulled the car forward six inches until the edge of the door caught between a break in the barriers, then reversed, lodging the door into place. He climbed out and took three steps back, readying the axe mattock for combat. The pack slammed into the door. The barrier held, buying them precious seconds.

Rushing past the young woman, he handed her the crow-bar. "Follow me."

At the Smithsfield Street Bridge, Paul paused to catch his breath and check out the area. The situation on the north side of the river was growing worse by the minute. Screams, snarling, and gunfire echoed from the city, and more pillars of black smoke lofted skyward. He could not see the bridge surface from the parkway, but it had to be better than heading into Pittsburgh. It remained the only option, especially since three of the deaders had climbed over the Prius and rushed toward them.

"Velma, follow me."

"My name is Daphne."

Paul cocked an eye. "Seriously?"

It took a second for her to get the reference. "Fuck you."

Daphne climbed the guardrail from Pitt-Lincoln Parkway onto Fort Pitt Boulevard. Paul followed, making it to the street as the deaders reached their location. Thank God none of them could climb. He hoped.

Vehicles jammed the intersection connecting the boulevard with the bridge. Bodies littered the area, most so badly eaten they could not reanimate. The few that could crawled along the cement. Deaders wandered through the cars, oblivious to the food hiding nearby. Traffic snarled the inbound lanes of the bridge while those heading south had no vehicles on them. A handful of deaders meandered through the vehicles in the northbound lanes.

Paul leaned closer to Daphne. "We're going to cross the bridge. Stay low and be quiet. They won't notice us. Ready?"

Daphne nodded.

Leading the way, Paul and Daphne raced through the intersection and on to the bridge. None of the deaders noticed them. Hopefully, their luck would hold out until they reached the other side. Staying low and close to the guardrail, the two made their way along the sidewalk to the other side.

As they passed by a school bus, a cacophony of snarls and the slamming of hands against glass greeted them. An outbreak had occurred on the bus, turning everyone on board into the living dead. A dozen elementary school deaders tried to get at them. The noise attracted the attention of the other deaders on the bridge. They glanced around and, on spotting the new prey, rushed toward Paul and Daphne.

"Run."

Daphne did not need to be told twice.

Paul glanced over his shoulder after a hundred feet. The three fastest deaders were almost upon him. The closest wore a FedEx uniform, the skin and muscles chewed off its right arm and neck. It headed straight for Paul. He swung the axe side of the mattock, driving the blade deep into the side of the FedEx deaders head. The left side of its head caved in and its jaw detached, hanging grotesquely. It toppled over to one side, thrashing around on the cement.

The second deader, a woman in a blood-stained pink jogging outfit, was already upon him. Paul held the mattock in front of him and slammed the handle against its chest, pushing it back several feet. He stepped forward, placed his right leg behind the deader's left leg, and shoved again. It fell backward onto the bridge. Paul drove the axe blade into its face. It cleaved the lower portion of the deader's head, burying itself into the brain stem. The deader stopped moving.

The third deader, this one a truck driver with a gore-encrusted beard and a piece of flesh dangling from its mouth, charged Daphne. She drove the end of the crowbar up and into its chest, rupturing its heart and impaling it on the metal. It still reached for her. Luckily, Daphne had enough sense not to release her grip on the crowbar. Paul rushed over and slammed the hammer portion of the mattock on to the top of its skull. The truck driver's head exploded on impact. Using his left foot, Paul pushed the deader off the end of the crowbar. It collapsed onto the bridge.

"Headshots are the only the only thing that works against them."

"Thanks."

The other six deaders were getting closer. One in casual clothes with its guts hanging out of its torn open abdomen and a second in a leather bra and mini-skirt, and hobbled by a broken ankle, were at the rear of the pack and posed no immediate threat. The other four were closing in.

Paul moved toward a male deader naked from the waist up, most of the skin on its torso chewed off, and smashed the business end of the mattock into its face. It dropped to the ground. Paul moved toward the next deader, this one an EMT with large chunks ripped out of its neck and right arm. He swung the bladed portion of the mattock against its neck, tearing it open down to the spinal column. Removing the blade, this time he aimed for the back of its neck. The second blow lopped off its head. The head rolled down the bridge as the body crumbled into a bloody heap. Paul returned to the half-naked deader, which was trying to stand. He brought the blade down on its neck, decapitating it with a single blow.

Two deaders went after Daphne. The first, an Asian man with its left arm missing, reached out for her. Daphne drove the pointed end of the crowbar into its left eye, shoved the weapon until it struck the back of the skull, and twisted. As its brain scrambled, its snarl devolved into a mewl.

The second deader, wearing a biker's leather pants and jacket, rushed forward and tackled Daphne, knocking her down. The crowbar flew out of her hands and clattered onto the cement. It climbed on top of her, going for her neck. Daphne balled her hands into fists and placed them under its chin, holding the deader away from her.

"I need some help."

Paul ran over. He did not want to use the mattock out of fear of hurting Daphne. Instead, he dropped it, grabbed the deader by the collar of its leather jacket, and pulled the biker off her. It lashed out, trying to reach the food. Using his free hand to grab the bottom of its jacket, Paul dragged the biker over to the side of the bridge and tossed it over the guardrail onto the train tracks below.

Paul turned to Daphne. "Are you—"

Daphne had already picked up the crowbar and was using

it to pound the head of the deader with its guts hanging out. Paul smiled. She might make a good apocalypse partner after all. Grabbing the mattock, he walked over and beheaded the female in the skimpy leather outfit. Thankfully, the melee had not attracted any other deaders to them.

Adrenaline pumped through his body, heightening all his senses. He hoped it would not stop anytime soon. The last thing he needed was the crash after such a rush if he hoped to get them out of this mess. He breathed heavy from the exertion and his shoulder blade ached.

"We need to find a place to hold up for a few minutes, catch our breath, and figure out our next course of action."

"Sounds good to me," Daphne gasped. "There are a lot of small businesses on this side of the bridge. We can find a place there."

The pair made their way to the southern ramp. Carnage had taken place on this side of the river, but nowhere near the level in Pittsburgh. Paul spotted only two deaders, one with broken legs that dragged itself away from them and another two hundred feet down the street banging on the window of a store, presumably trying to get to someone trapped inside. Seven bodies stripped of flesh and muscles lay scattered on the street. Abandoned vehicles sat at various angles. Most of the small businesses within sight were family-run restaurants that had borne the brunt of the outbreak. Windows were smashed, outdoor tables overturned, and blood and body parts scattered everywhere. Even if Paul considered sheltering in one of the glass-fronted eateries, a fire raged inside a seafood restaurant in the center of the block. Within ten minutes, the entire string of restaurants would be in flames. Only one place made a good safe haven. On one of the side streets, he saw a sign over the sidewalk advertising Jack Nasty's. Paul doubted a location with that name would have windows in it.

The two made their way to a plumber's van in the middle of the street and hugged the side. Paul scanned the area to make certain no deaders were around. The area was clear. As he moved alongside the van, a deader pushed through the driver's side window, snarling and grasping for him. Paul raised the mattock and brought the axe down on its head. The top of the skull shattered, the fragments dropping into the street. A moment later, its brain slid out and hit the asphalt with a sickening plop.

Paul led Daphne down the center of the side street. As he predicted, Jack Nasty's was inside an old brick building with the Masonic emblem carved in stone on the second floor. Wooden boards covered the windows on the first floor with XXX painted on the wall to the left of the door and Live Nude Girls on the right. Beneath the Masonic emblem, someone had painted a burning skull in a top hat encircled by the slogan Liquor in the Front, Poker in the Rear.

"Figures you'd pick this place," quipped Daphne.

"Don't get all high and mighty on me. It's the safest place to hold out in for a while."

"I'm not taking my clothes off for you."

Paul smiled at the prospect.

Droplets of blood stained the sidewalk in front of the strip club. Paul pushed on the door. It was unlocked. He stepped inside the dimly lit alcove and listened. No sounds came from inside. Daphne stood by the doors, propping one open on her shoulder and scanning the area for danger.

He moved beside her and whispered, "I think it's clear inside. We're going in but be ready to run."

Paul held the mattock in his left hand and removed the Glock from its holster. Daphne brandished the crowbar like a baseball bat. They stepped through the double doors of the foyer into the club.

A stripper in chaps and cowboy boots lunged at them.

Chapter Four

THE STRIPPER MADE it only a few feet when it was yanked to a stop. It had been ravaged, its breasts eaten off and its abdomen torn open. The intestines had fallen out. The loose end had become entangled around the stripper pole, limiting its movement.

Paul chucked. "This is like something from a bad movie."

"It's not funny." Daphne stepped forward and plunged the pointed end of the crowbar into the deader's eye socket, churning it around until she scrambled its brain. The stripper dropped to the floor.

"Hello?" Paul yelled.

"What are you doing?"

"Making sure we're alone." When he heard no sounds from anywhere in the club, he called out again. "Is anyone in here?"

Nothing.

"I think we're safe for now. Go lock the front doors so no one sneaks in."

Daphne frowned but exited into the foyer. Paul switched on the interior lights.

The outbreak must have occurred in here as well. Eight bodies, three strippers and five patrons, lay strewn across the floor. All of them had shotgun wounds to the chest and head. Blood covered the floor and stage, making the footing slippery. He wandered through the chaos.

Daphne returned. "I bolted the door but it won't hold up long if those pile up outside. What are you doing?"

"Looking for this." Paul crouched down and lifted off the floor a Vepr twelve-gauge semi-automatic shotgun covered in blood. He brought it behind the bar, picked up a cloth, and wiped down the shotgun. Checking under the counter, he found exactly what he wanted–a spare box of shells and six small bottles of spring water.

Daphne had found a table in the corner near the exit not covered in gore. Paul brought his find over, placed them on the surface, and handed a bottle of water to Daphne.

"Drink this."

"Thanks." She twisted off the cap and swigged half of it in one gulp.

Paul did the same. For the first time since this nightmare began, he felt his breathing and heart rate return to normal.

He thought of his soon-to-be-ex-wife Alissa. She worked at Mass General Hospital in Boston and was probably caught in the middle of her own outbreak. He removed his cellphone from his trouser pocket. The screen had cracks running along it but remained functional, though his power had dropped to twenty-three percent. Paul called up his contact list and dialed Alissa's number.

The irritating three-tone warning blared from the speaker followed by a pre-recorded message that all lines were busy so please try again later. Paul disconnected the call and tried again with the same results.

"Are you trying to call your family?" asked Daphne.

"No."

"Girlfriend?"

"My ex-wife. She's a nurse in Boston. We own a cabin in New Hampshire. I wanted to know if she planned on heading there."

"Do you think a cabin in the woods is safe?"

"This one is stocked with enough food, water, and ammunition to last months."

Daphne's eyes widened. "Is that where you're heading?"

"That's where we're heading, if you want to join me."

"I'd like that. It's better than staying in Pittsburgh."

"Shouldn't you be trying to reach your family?"

"I left my cellphone in my car."

Paul held out his. "You can use mine."

"I don't have anyone to call. My mother died when I was eight and I haven't talked to my father or brothers in ten years."

"Boyfriend?"

Daphne shook her head.

Paul tried one more time to call Alissa but could not get through. Instead, he typed a text message.

STUCK IN PITTSBURGH. SHIT HIT THE FAN HERE. AM HEADING FOR THE CABIN. I ADVISE YOU DO THE SAME. SITUATION OUT OF CONTROL. MAY BE ONLY SAFE SPOT. IF YOU GET THERE BEFORE ME, PASSWORD IS YOUR BIRTH-DAY IN EIGHT NUMBERS. GOOD LUCK AND TRUST NO ONE.

Paul hit the send button, hoping his text would so through. He turned off the power to his cellphone and slid it back into his pocket.

He then checked out the shotgun. It was empty. Ejecting the magazine, he loaded twelve rounds from the box then inserted it back into the shotgun.

"So, is Macho the Magnificent going to hoard all the guns for himself or do I get one?"

"I'm Paul."

"Daphne." She sneered. "But you know that already."

"I'm sorry."

"That's okay. I know I look like a sexed-up version of Velma. I shouldn't be mad at you. It's just…. I'd be dead by now if not for you. I should be thanking you."

"Don't worry about it. You saved my life, too. I never could have fought off the deaders by myself. Friends?"

"Deader fighting buddies for now." Daphne motioned

toward the shotgun. "Am I going to get a weapon?"

Paul stood and removed the police utility belt from around his waist, placing it on the table in front of Daphne. She removed the sidearm and aimed it at the wall, looking down the sight. Paul noticed her finger rested on the outside of the weapon and not on the trigger.

"You know how to use one of those?"

"Surprised?"

"A little."

"My dad belonged to the NRA. He was an abusive asshole, but at least he taught me how to shoot." She examined the weapon. "Where's the safety?"

"It's a Glock 23. The safety is in the trigger."

"Sweet." Daphne slid the Glock back into it holster. "Where do we go from here?"

"Our only chance of surviving is to get as far away from the city as fast as possible. I saw some cars in the parking lot. We could steal one and head south."

Daphne shook her head. "There's nothing south of us but residential neighborhoods. We wouldn't get far before we were overrun."

"I saw a marina as we crossed the bridge. It's close to here. We could grab a boat and head downriver."

"I hope you know how to drive one because I don't."

"They must have a small motorboat that's easy to operate. Even a canoe. As long as we get away from here."

"Count me in."

Paul checked his watch. It was twelve minutes after four. "I want to get to the marina before it gets dark. But first...."

Placing the mattock on the table, he grabbed the shotgun and stood.

"Where are you going?"

"I want to check out this place to see if there are any survivors or other things we can use."

Daphne stood and buckled the belt around her waist. "You're not leaving me here alone."

Chapter Five

O THER THAN THE club room, the first floor was empty. The restrooms were unoccupied and the kitchen abandoned. They found uncooked food in the freezer, which did them no good. The changing room brought better luck. Two of the girls used backpacks as purses. Paul emptied them. They could carry their water and spare ammunition. He gave one to Daphne. He found a thin, black leather jacket draped over one of the dressing chairs and handed it to Daphne.

"Try this on."

She grinned. "Pervert."

"Deaders can't bite through leather. It might save your life."

Daphne slid on the jacket and zipped it up. It was snug around her chest but other than that, fit perfectly.

They climbed the stairs to the second floor. It contained four small rooms on the left for those girls willing to go the extra mile for a few more dollars and an office at the far end. Paul knocked on the first door. No one answered, so he opened it. Daphne gasped.

The body of a stripper lay naked on the blood-soaked bed. Someone had beaten her face so severely it had caved in. A chunk of flesh from a hairy arm lay beside her head. She must have turned during sex and bitten her client, to which he responded by beating her to death. A biker's outfit sat in the corner and a pool of blood stained the center of the floor, with a crimson trail leading out into the hall. Chances were good they would find his naked corpse amongst the pile of corpses downstairs. Paul used a sheet to cover the stripper's upper body. He and Daphne exited back into the hall. The next three rooms were empty.

Upon reaching the office, Paul knocked. No one answered. He tried the knob but it was locked. Standing back, he kicked just above the knob. The door burst open and slammed against the wall. A lone figure sat behind the desk, a fat man whose dirty polo shirt strained against his massive stomach. Paul raised the shotgun to defend them but lowered it. This guy ranked among the dead. He had placed a gun in his mouth and pulled the trigger rather than face the clusterfuck in his club. The only portion that remained was the dangling lower jaw. The remainder had splattered across the wall to his rear.

Paul entered the room and crossed over to the desk as Daphne stood watch in the doorway.

"What are you looking for?" she asked.

"Whatever he shot himself with. The more firepower we have, the better our... bingo."

Paul reached down and lifted a .357 Magnum off the floor. He placed it on the desk and rummaged through the drawers. He found a Ziploc bag filled with marijuana, another filled with Viagra pills, a bottle of Oxycodone, and a box of rounds for the Magnum. Placing the loot on the desk, he picked up the revolver, flipped open the chamber, and filled the empty slot from the box. Paul slipped the Magnum between his pants and his back, placed the other items in the backpack, and rejoined Daphne.

Daphne grinned. "I saw what you put in the backpack. Planning on a party later?"

"They're for bartering in case we run across someone willing to trade."

Once downstairs, Paul placed the bottles of water and one of Jack Daniels in the backpack and zipped it close. He then checked the bodies for a leather jacket he could wear. Sure enough, he found the naked guy with a large chunk taken out of his face among the dead, but no leather jackets. He opted for a thick denim jacket two sizes too large. At least it would prevent him from being bitten. Next, he rummaged through the dead for a pair of boots since the expensive loafers he wore would not last long. After trying on several pair, he opted for brown, ankle-high work boots that fit him perfectly. They smelled of sweaty feet, but he did not care. The smell coming from the living dead was far worse.

Paul picked up the mattock in his left hand while holding the shotgun in his right.

"Are you ready?"

Daphne made a clicking sound with her mouth and pointed her forefinger at him.

"If anything happens to me, take the shotgun, Magnum, and backpack and keep running. Let's go."

Chapter Six

THE SITUATION OUTSIDE had not changed. The street was clear of deaders. Paul led the way back to the intersection and paused to check the area. The lone deader still stood in front of the store trying to get in. Nothing stood between them and the marina.

They ran out into the center of the street and headed west. A sign off to their right read The Landing and Marina at Station Square. Paul veered off and raced down the cement walkway, constantly on the lookout for danger.

As they passed the club bar, snarling and scratching on glass caught their attention. Fifteen deaders stood inside trying to get at them through the glass doors.

"Keep going. Those doors won't hold them for long."

Halfway across the causeway, a male deader in flip flops and a Hawaiian shirt wandering on the docks heard their footsteps and charged. Paul kept running until it was twenty feet away. He stopped, raised the shotgun, and fired a single round that obliterated the deader's head. Forward momentum kept it going. Paul jumped out of the way as it crashed onto the causeway in a bloody heap, then he and Daphne continued onto the dock.

The first row berthed three cabin cruisers. Paul by passed them for the next dock that moored two cabin cruisers, a sailboat, and, at the far end, a small four-seater. He headed for that.

The shattering of glass echoed across the marina. The

combined weight of the deaders had broken the twin doors. Deaders fell through, creating a pile of living dead. Three stood and raced down the causeway toward them. Paul and Daphne had minutes to escape.

"Hold them off as long as you can."

Daphne centered herself on the dock, placed down her crowbar, and aimed the Glock. The first three deaders were still two hundred feet away and closing in. The remainder had stumbled to their feet and were heading down the causeway.

Paul jumped into the boat. Blood covered the steering wheel and driver's seat. The owner must have been attempting to escape when a deader took him out. Bad for the owner, a lucky break for them. The keys were in the ignition. He turned them into the on position and pressed the starter button. The engine roared to life.

The first deader, a middle-aged woman in a summer dress with the flesh chewed off both arms, rushed Daphne. She took careful aim and fired. The .40 caliber bullet tore its head off. It collapsed, tripping the deader behind it that stumbled to the side and fell into the river. The deader in the rear, wearing a waiter's uniform, jumped over the corpse and rushed her. Daphne panicked and fired three more times. The first two rounds impacted its chest and the third caught it between the eyes, blowing off the back of its skull and propelling the waiter deader backwards.

The remaining deaders reached the smaller dock and rushed Daphne.

"Get in!"

Paul ran to the stern and unfastened the mooring lines as Daphne picked up the crowbar and jumped in. Paul raced forward and pushed the throttle to full speed. The boat shot away from the dock.

Three deaders jumped the gap to get at their prey. Two hit the water and disappeared beneath the surface. The third landed on the stern, its leg dangling in the water, and started to climb aboard. Daphne holstered the Glock. Using the crowbar like a baseball bat, she swung it, connecting the curved end with the deader's face. Shattered teeth splayed across the river, yet it still held on. Daphne hammered at its hands until the deader lost its grip and dropped off the stern, sinking beneath the surface.

"All clear," she called out.

Paul maneuvered the boat into the middle of the river. Heading west was out of the question. The debris from the bridge and burning aviation fuel from the 737 blocked their path. He turned east and headed upriver.

"Hey!"

Paul glanced around but same nothing.

"Hey! Over here!"

Daphne tapped Paul's shoulder and pointed to the right. "There she is."

A woman stood on the last dock waving her arms above her head. "Please, don't leave me."

"We're not going to abandon her, are we?" asked Daphne.

"I'll do what I can."

Paul steered the boat toward her. The problem was that the remaining nine deaders had also heard the woman's plea and were racing down the dock toward her.

The boat was fifty feet from the end of the dock. Daphne yelled, "Swim for it."

"But you're so close."

Daphne pointed behind the woman. She turned and screamed. The deaders were closing in fast. The woman dove into the river and swam for her life, which did not last long. The deaders bounded off the end of the dock, splashing into the water around her. Three grabbed her as they sank, dragging her under. Paul maneuvered closer, hoping the woman would escape, but gave up when air bubbles and blood floated to the surface.

Daphne closed her eyes and mumbled a prayer.

Paul did not have time to mourn. He had to get them to safety while the outbreak was still in its early stage. Pushing the throttles forward, he spun the boat around and headed downriver.

Chapter Seven

THE RIVER VEERED south at the edge of Pittsburgh and meandered through the suburbs in a series of S-turns. Along both banks, the violence raged as furious as in the city. Screams, sirens, gunfire, and snarling echoed across the water. Columns of black smoke billowed from the neighborhoods on either side as well as farther down the river. Hundreds of people flocked to the safety of the waterway, followed by deaders. Most never made it to the banks. A few reached the relative safety of the river, only to swarmed by the living dead as they waded in. A handful who avoided the deaders swam toward their boat.

Paul throttled forward and sped down the river, swerving away from the survivors. Daphne gazed in horror as they swept by those clamoring to be saved. A construction worker swore at them as they passed. A mother begged them to save her and her two children. A middle-aged man, overweight and out of breath, slipped beneath the surface ten feet from them. A dozen people who could have been saved weren't.

Paul glanced over and saw the look of disgust on her face. "Are you okay?"

"No." Daphne's tone dropped with resignation. "I know we can't do anything. If we stop for one, we risk the others swarming the boat. It still bothers me, though."

Paul placed his hand gently on her shoulder and gave a reassuring squeeze. Daphne was right. They could not save everyone. To try would only get them killed. He realized it

27

could as easily be him and Daphne left out there to fend for themselves, and he wouldn't have blamed someone for the leaving him behind. The concept Paul had come to terms with years ago, and that Daphne had now discovered, is that when humanity died, all normal social concepts of decency had to die along with it if the survivors hoped to live. He found it difficult to put into practice, but he needed to if he wanted to make it back to New Hampshire.

Two wooded areas sat on either bank of the river. Paul gestured to the one on the left. "We'll land there. I need to find a map so we know where we're going."

"You don't want to do that. There are suburbs on either side of those trees. All you'll do is fight your way through residential neighborhoods."

"Shit."

"Keep going until you pass Route 70. The population gets smaller beyond the bridge."

Paul maneuvered the boat down the center of the river. Just south of Monessen and Charleroi, they reached the bridge. The towns were panic ridden. Survivors made their way to the banks only to be taken down at the river's edge or swim to the center where they had nowhere to go. A family of four attempting to escape in a canoe were swarmed by a pack of deaders that overturned them near the shore. By now, a stream of dead bodies floated along each bank of the river.

An explosion sounded off to their left. Paul and Daphne turned toward Monessen in time to see a giant fireball billowing into the sky. Thick, black smoke rose from the area. The roar of flames mingled with the screams of the living and the moans of the dead.

"What happened?" asked Daphne.

"A gas station must have blown up."

"Hopefully, it took a lot of deaders with it."

"Not nearly—"

"Watch out," warned Daphne.

A burly man, two hundred and fifty pounds of muscle, with long dark hair tied in a ponytail and a beard, swam toward them from the center of the river.

"Hey, buddy. Over here. Help me."

Paul accelerated and swung around him.

The man gave them both the finger. "Screw you, you motherfucking bastard."

Paul didn't care. His attention remained focused on the Route 70 bridge where carnage ensued.

Vehicles packed the span bumper to bumper and deaders filled every available space. People remained trapped in their cars, doomed to a slow death. Five survivors had made it to the roof of a U-Haul truck with scores of the living dead surrounding them, clutching at the bay to reach the food. A teenage couple saw the boat approaching and tried to make it safety by jumping into the river. The male scanned the gap and plunged into the water never to resurface. He was the lucky one. His female companion slammed chest first into the guardrail and bounced back onto the bridge. Within seconds, a pack of deaders descended on her, tearing the girl apart.

Even worse, the failed escape alerted the deaders to the boat drawing near. They swarmed the edge along the northern expanse, reaching over and grasping at Paul and Daphne. One of the deaders leaned too far over and plummeted off the bridge, smashing face first into the river. More of the living dead joined in until dozens dropped into the river.

"I don't believe this," said Daphne. "It's raining deaders."

Paul pushed the throttles to full and headed for the center span. The deaders above became frantic, even more falling over the side.

"What are you doing?" Daphne asked.

"Trust me."

Fifty feet before the bridge, Paul swerved hard left toward the bank for several seconds, then hard right under the span, passing by the deader waterfall.

A thud came from the rear of the boat. They both turned around. A female deader in a blue summer dress had landed on the back seat. It tried to stand, hampered by the femur extending through the skin.

"I got this." Daphne picked up the crowbar and moved toward the stern.

The female deader had risen, using its good leg. Daphne swung the crowbar like a baseball bat, the curved end connecting with the side of its head. It spun around and fell against the transom, its upper half hanging over the stern and its legs still inside the boat. Dropping the crowbar, Daphne grabbed the deader by the ankles and tossed it over the side before returning to Paul.

"Thanks."

"You were busy." Daphne nudged him in the arm. "Isn't it sad that stuff like that doesn't bother me anymore?"

"Trust me. It's going to get worse."

THEY CONTINUED FOR another thirty minutes until they reached the Route 40 bridge and the town of Brownsville. Both were silent and, at least from the perspective of the river, contained neither the living nor living dead.

Paul passed a cement outcrop on the left that served as the terminus of the town's rainwater drainage system and circled back to it, pulling the boat alongside. He stopped and shut off the engine.

"Is this where we get off?" asked Daphne.

"It's only a pit stop. I want to raid that before we go on."

Paul motioned to a small service station/quickie mart visible on the opposite side of the road. He emptied the backpack and placed the contents on one of the seats.

"That place doesn't look ransacked and there don't appear to be any deaders around. I'm going over to stock up on supplies. We'll need them if we hope to get to New Hampshire."

"What about me?"

"You stay here with the boat."

"Because you don't trust me?"

"No. I need someone to keep an eye on the boat. If we lose it, we're screwed. If anyone or anything shows up, park yourself in the middle of the river. If I'm not back in thirty minutes, go on without me."

Daphne shook her head. "I'll give you an hour."

"If I'm not back in thirty minutes, there's a good chance I'm not coming back at all."

Paul slung the shotgun and empty backpack over his shoulders, took the crowbar, and climbed up on the drainage outlet.

Chapter Eight

PAUL MADE HIS way up to the embankment, crouching at the edge of the twin railroad tracks running along the river. Nothing moved along them, so he raced ahead to the rear of the building opposite the service station and peered around the rear corner. A pair of deaders stood in front of the glass window, scratching at the surface. That meant only one thing—there was at least one survivor inside. Taking those two out would be easy, especially with their attention drawn away from him.

Creeping along the side of the building, Paul stopped at the front corner and scanned the streets. He saw nothing but a brindle-colored stray boxer, probably wondering what had happened to its master.

Brandishing the crowbar with the pointed side out, he rushed across the street and drove the end into the back of the closest deader's head, driving the edge up at the point where the neck connected to the skull. It penetrated three inches. Paul drove it in deeper and churned. The deader convulsed for a second before going limp, sliding off the crowbar.

The second deader spun around to face him. It was an Asian man in its mid-forties with the right side of its head and neck chewed off. It growled at Paul. He slammed the edge of the crowbar into its face, gouging out one eye and stunning it. Swinging the crowbar around, he shoved the curved end into its mouth and twisted up. The front of the Asian deader's skull tore open, ripping off everything from its upper jaw to its forehead and splattering Paul in gore. He wiped the human detritus off his face and spit as the deader collapsed to the cement.

"Iso," someone cried from inside the store. An attractive Asian woman in her mid-thirties knelt by the glass, her hands pressed against its surface as she stared at her husband and sobbed. A boy approximately fourteen stood behind her offering what comfort he could.

Shit. He had killed their loved one in front of them. Not a way to make a good first impression.

Paul pushed on the door but it would not open.

"Unlock it," he said softly.

The boy stepped around his mother, unlocked it, and pulled open the door. Paul stepped inside, locking it behind him.

A scraggily looking kid in his late teens pushed past the mother and son and ran up to Paul. His blonde hair was unwashed. He wore sneakers, jeans, and a black T-shirt that had seen better days, the latter straining against a slight paunch. Paul took an immediate dislike to him.

"Get me outa here."

"Calm down, Sparky." Paul placed a hand on the kid's chest and pushed him back. "Women and children first."

"Screw them. They're the reason I'm trapped here."

Paul gave the kid a stare that silenced him. Sparky backed off and averted his gaze.

"What's going on here?"

The teenager answered for his mother who still wept for her husband. "I'm Toshii. My mother is Akiko. We're on vacation from Japan. We were getting gas when the rising began. My father fought off several of the dead while my mother and I escaped into here."

"We almost didn't make it thanks to him." Akiko pointed at Sparky.

"He tried to lock us out," added Toshii.

"Why?" snapped Paul as he spun around to face Sparky.

"It's a crisis. Every man for himself."

"Listen, Sparky—"

"My name is Clem."

"Whatever. You keep away from me or I'll break your leg and leave you here."

"You wouldn't dare."

Paul brandished the crowbar and stepped toward Sparky. The kid raised his hands and jumped back.

"All right, man. Sorry."

"How did you get here?" asked Akiko.

"I have a boat. I came here—"

"If you have a boat let's get out of here," said Sparky.

"I came here to get supplies, so calm down."

"But we need to go now while we have the chance."

"I doubt there are any deaders left." Akiko dried her eyes and stood, clutching her son tight. "Most of the residents headed south. The dead followed them. The only reason those two stayed is because they knew we were in here."

"Who is the other one?"

Toshii pointed to Sparky. "His boss. He went out to help us and got killed by the dead."

Paul spun around to face the kid. "Didn't you try to help?"

"And get eaten? No way."

"Get this straight, asshole. *If* I decide to save you, no more of this shit. I'm in charge. You listen to me and become a team player or I'll leave you behind."

Sparky became defiant. "You can't tell me what to do."

Paul responded by unslinging his shotgun and aiming it inches from Sparky's face. "Have it your way."

"Jesus, all right. Calm the fuck down. I'll do anything to get out of here."

"I don't doubt that." Paul slung the shotgun over his shoulder. "You, stand in the corner and don't move. Akiko, you and Toshii get in the other corner where you're safe."

As they responded, Paul made the rounds of the store, filling the backpack with water, packages of beef jerky, and canned food.

DAPHNE KEPT SCANNING the bank for signs of deaders or survivors. She spotted neither.

The moaning of deaders came from the distance. Daphne turned around. A horde of forty to fifty deaders lined the opposite bank of the river. They must have heard them pull up earlier because their eyes focused on her. Thank God they were on the other side otherwise Paul would be screwed.

One deader jumped in the water and attempted to swim across. Its dead brain prevented it from using its limbs properly. The thing struggled to stay afloat before disappearing beneath the surface and floating down stream.

A second deader tried to cross, but rather than swimming it kept walking until it disappeared beneath the surface. A minute later, the rest of the horde did the same thing until they were out of sight. At least they were persistent if not bright. She only hoped that they could—

Something jumped into the boat behind her. Daphne spun around and withdrew the Glock. She recognized the pony-tailed biker they had avoided awhile ago. He lunged, punching her in the jaw and sending her sprawling back against the control board. Daphne aimed the Glock. Before she could pull the trigger, the biker clutched her wrist with his left hand and twisted the gun away from her with his right. A bolt of pain raced down her forefinger. He threw the Glock onto the passenger seat and punch Daphne in the abdomen, knocking the wind out of her.

"Fucking bitch. You and your pussy boyfriend thought you could leave me behind? Well, guess what? The boat's mine now."

The biker grabbed Daphne by the hair, dragged her to the stern, and through her on the cushioned bench. Daphne tried to catch her breath but couldn't. He stood over her, unzipped his pants, and pulled out his erection.

"Before I kill you, I'm going to make you sorry for leaving me behind."

Chapter Nine

T HE BIKER GRABBED Daphne by the belt and yanked, trying to pull down her pants. She fought back, kicking at his groin and pounding on his chest. He released his grip long enough to punch her again in the mouth, almost dislocating the jaw. Daphne lashed out again. This time she extended her fingers, dug the nails into his cheek, and ripped off a chunk of skin.

"Cunt!" The biker punched Daphne two more times in the abdomen, knocking the fight out of her. She struggled to regain her energy as the biker fought to get the pants off her. Daphne was only semi-unconscious when the sound of swirling water attracted her attention. She gazed to the right.

All around the boat, the deaders from the other side of the river broke through the surface and strolled onto the bank. Most staggered inland. Five heard her and the biker struggling in the boat and charged. When they crawled up on the cement drainage system, Daphne summoned what energy she could and kicked the biker in the balls, then lifted her legs and shoved him against the gunwale. Two deaders grabbed him, one biting his arm and the other tearing a chunk out his neck. They pulled the biker out of the boat onto the drainage system. He screamed and flailed, unable to escape as they fed on him. The remaining three crawled over the frenzy trying to get at her.

Daphne jumped up and raced to the front, falling against the rear of the driver's seat. She slid around to the front, started the engine, and throttled forward. The boat pulled away from the drainage system as the three deaders jumped. One bounced off the stern and rolled over the side, its head churned into chum by the propellor. The other two landed in the back, falling to their knees.

Daphne maneuvered the boat into the center of the river. When the deaders stood, Daphne spun the steering wheel hard left. The boat lurched to one side. The deader in a post office uniform lost balance, stumbled to starboard, and tumbled into the river. The second, a female in a gore-soaked cheerleader outfit, staggered but clutched onto the back of one of the seats at the last second. Daphne throttled back, giving the deader time to regain its footing. When it did, Daphne pushed the engines to full. The boat lurched forward, sending the deader sprawling on the rear bench.

Daphne stopped the boat, jumped up, and grabbed the Glock the biker had thrown on the passenger seat. She raced to the back and attempted to aim, finding it difficult due to the rocking of the boat. The cheerleader deader jumped off the seat and charged. Daphne pulled the trigger. The first round struck it in the chest, the hollow point blowing its lungs and heart across the stern, the concussion throwing it back. Daphne leaned against the front seat to steady herself. When it attacked a second time, she fired twice, one bullet catching the deader in the throat and the second above its eyes. It collapsed to the deck. Daphne moved over and finished it off with a final bullet to the face. She would dispose of the body later.

Turning her attention to the riverbank, she noticed the pair of deaders still feeding on the biker. They had stripped him of most of his flesh and muscles. He would not reanimate. The remaining thirty wandered inland, heading toward the service station Paul had gone to.

PAUL FINISHED STUFFING the backpack to the point he could

barely zip it shut. The damned thing weighed a ton, but at least they had enough to eat and drink for the next few days as well as basic medical supplies. Removing two maps from the counter, a spindled map of all fifty states and a folded one of the northeast, he slid those into the outer pockets. He hefted the backpack over his left shoulder and the shotgun over his right, shifted the balance, then grabbed the crowbar.

"We're all set. I have a boat down by the river that'll take us to safety."

"We're going to have trouble getting there." Toshii pointed to the window.

Thirty deaders staggered up the street leading from the river and spread out along the main street by the station, oblivious to the food nearby. Paul's first thought focused on Daphne's safety.

"Everyone down." Paul pushed Akiko and Toshii behind the counter and crouched.

Sparky opted to save his own skin. He raced for the door and pushed it open, hoping to make a break. The ringing of the bell on the upper jamb caught the horde's attention. The deaders snarled and lunged at the fresh meat. Sparky stood frozen in the doorway.

Paul had no qualms about letting the horde take out Sparky. The kid was useless. But letting Sparky die also meant letting the dead inside. Rushing to the front of the station, Paul yanked the kid back inside, then closed and locked the glass door. As he stepped back and armed himself with the shotgun, the horde slammed into the plate glass. Paul prayed it would hold.

Thankfully, it did.

Akiko crouched in front of the counter, hidden from view of the deaders and shaking in terror. Toshii comforted her.

"Come on," said Sparky. "There's a door in the storeroom. We can get out that way."

Paul shook his head. "We'll never make it past them to the

river."

"The fast ones will."

For a moment, Paul considering shooting Sparky in the leg and leaving him as bait. Instead, he crossed the station and opened the door to the mechanic's bay. The scratching and banging on the glass told him he had only seconds to find a way out.

The mechanic's bay held two spaces for repair. Both were in use. A Ford pick-up truck rested on the raised vehicle lift against the far wall and a Nissan two-door sat on the raised lift in front of him. Paul had figured out their escape route. Sure, it was insane and wouldn't work, but it beat standing around waiting to die. He checked the wall beside him and found what he needed.

"Sparky, get in here."

The kid poked his head through the door. "What?"

Paul pointed to the center of the rear wall. "Stand there."

"Why?"

"I need someone as bait."

"No fucking way, man."

"You got us into this mess. You're going to help us get out of it."

"I'll take me chances out back." Sparky ran away and disappeared into the storeroom.

Toshii rushed past Paul and stood against the wall. Akiko ran after him. Paul stopped her from entering the bay.

"It'll be okay. It's our only chance."

Paul heard the plate glass crack.

Paul pressed the button that raised the farthest of the bay doors. As predicted, the whir of the engine and clanking of metal attracted the deaders' attention. Seconds later, the first of the horde raced into the bay and swarmed toward him and Toshii. Toshii waved his hands and yelled to get their attention. When they were only feet away, Paul pressed two more buttons. The twin lifts dropped, catching twenty of the living dead and crushing them under the combined weight of the lifts and vehicles. The crunching of bones filled the bay, followed by a horizontal spray of blood and organs as their bodies ruptured.

Three survived. The first, a male deader in gym shorts and a t-shirt, hesitated between Paul and Toshii. The indecision gave Paul enough time to blast away its head. A female deader in casual clothes rushed between the two vehicles toward Toshii while a naked male deader circled behind the Nissan aiming for Paul. Paul rushed over to Toshii, shielding the teenager, and took down the female deader with a single shot to the face. Switching targets, he blasted the naked male deader, tearing off its head and covering Akiko in blood and gore.

"Follow me."

Paul moved past the Nissan with Akiko and Toshii close behind. A deader with a broken leg emerged in the open bay. He blasted off its head and stepped outside.

Sparky ran past the other end of the station and headed for the safety of the river. The remaining nine deaders in front of the door noticed him and gave chase, providing the distraction they needed. Motioning for the other two to follow, Paul headed for the right side of the building across the street and sprinted to the boat.

DAPHNE HEARD THE commotion in the street followed by gunfire. At least she knew Paul was still alive. But for how long?

Eight deaders stood along the riverbank, clutching for her. The earlier gunfire that had killed the biker drew the attention of the horde that had crossed the river. Not a problem. Daphne maneuvered the boat a hundred yards upriver and revved the engine. The eight deaders chased after her. Daphne ignored them, keeping her eyes out for Paul. A brindle-colored Boxer emerged from the behind one of the buildings and ran toward the river, barking furiously. Farther down, a scraggy-looking guy with nine deaders in tow appeared from the center of town. Upon seeing the boat, he ran toward her. Now she had seventeen deaders to deal with.

Knowing he would never outrun the dead, the scraggly-looking guy dove into the river and swam. Three deaders followed, disappearing beneath the surface. Still no sign of—

Paul emerged from behind one of the buildings along with a mother and her teenage son. Daphne continued revving the engine to draw the deaders' attention. Now the two who had been feeding off the biker charged. Paul made for the gap between the two packs and waved for Daphne to meet him there.

Daphne spun the boat around and headed for shore, nearly running over the scraggly-looking guy. He cursed at her as she passed. Fuck him. She brought the boat in as close as possible and waited.

PAUL NOTICED THE two packs of deaders closing in on each side. He glanced over his shoulder. Akiko and Toshii were tight behind him. This would be close. Some from the larger pack waded into the river after Sparky. At least he was finally good for something.

At the river's edge, Paul paused and dropped the crowbar. "Get on board. I'll cover you."

The larger pack was closer. Paul fired the Vepr low at the lead deader, ripping away its right leg. It collapsed. The next four deaders stumbled over it, buying him a few seconds. He continued firing into the pack as it drew nearer.

Daphne pulled Akiko over the gunwale. "Get your son."

As Akiko pulled Toshii aboard, Daphne withdrew the Glock and fired at the two deaders approaching Paul from behind. She used up the rest of the magazine taking down one of them, then switched out the magazine for a full one.

"Paul, behind you."

Paul spun around and fired a single round into the last deader's head, splattering it across the grass. He had expended his last round. Flinging the shotgun over his shoulder, he unholstered the Magnum and used it against the remaining seven deaders, aligning his aim carefully. He had only six rounds. Four went down with headshots. One bullet blew open the chest on a fifth deader. The last missed completely.

Daphne finished reloading and fired on the last two deaders, eventually hitting one with two shots to the head and putting a bullet into the upper skull of the last. It staggered and fell. Akiko had pulled Toshii to safety. Daphne holstered the Glock and ran to the controls.

"Hurry up."

Picking up the crowbar, Paul waded to the boat and tossed it inside. Grabbing the gunwale, he pulled himself in. Toshii helped, clutching the back of Paul's shirt and lifting.

"Watch out!" yelled Akiko.

The last deader hit in the skull only had the top half of its brain shot off. It jumped to its feet and lunged at Paul, wrapping its arms around his waist and dragging him back into the river. Toshii nearly tumbled over the side, Akiko yanking him back at the last second.

Paul did not have time to take a breath before going under. His lungs already ached for air. The deader positioned itself on top of him, pinning him to bottom. It tried to bite Paul's face, its movement slowed by the water. Paul raised his right arm and the deader sunk its teeth into his wrist, thrashing like a shark to rip off a chunk of flesh. Its knee fell onto Paul's chest, forcing from his lungs what little air remained. Paul involuntarily breathed in, panicking as his lungs filled with water. What a way to go. To be drowned and then devoured.

The deader fell off Paul. Without the weight, he kicked his way to the surface, grabbed the gunwale with his left hand, and tried to breathe. His lungs filled with water. Two pairs of hands grabbed him under each armpit and lifted him inside. He fell on his knees, gasping and hacking. His lungs convulsed and he heaved river water onto the deck. Air poured into his lungs, causing him to convulse and spit out more water.

Glancing to his left, he noticed the Boxer he had spotted earlier attacking the deader. It had dived into the water, bit the collar of its shirt, and dragged the thing off Paul, saving his life. The dog pulled the deader up the bank, avoiding the clutching hands that reached over its head. Toshii pulled the Glock out of Daphne's holster and fired a round into the deader's chest. The bullet had no impact but did succeed in scaring off the Boxer. Once the dog was clear, Toshii put two rounds into the deader's head.

Toshii tapped the side of the boat. "Come here, boy."

The Boxer ran into the water and swam over to them. Toshii tried to lift it in but did not have the strength. His mother came over to help and the two eventually pulled the dog inside. The Boxer barked once and, with its stub tail wagging, stepped over to the boy and rubbed against him.

Daphne swung the boat into the middle of the river and stopped, then ran back to check on Paul. He lay on his hands and knees, still struggling for air and hacking up water and bile. He would live. She placed her hand on his back and rubbed.

"Are you okay?"

Paul gave her a thumbs up then leaned forward to hack the last of the water out of his lungs. After that, his breathing came easier. After inhaling several times, he stood, using the seats to support himself. He steadied himself as his heart rate gradually returned to normal.

"What happened?" Paul gasped.

"One of the deaders attacked you but he saved you." Toshii motioned to the dog.

"Thanks." Paul reached out to pet the dog. It ran over, wagging its stub tail and barking once as Paul scratched the dog behind its ears.

"Can we keep him?" Toshii asked excitedly.

"No," answered Akiko. "This nice man can't rescue all of us."

Toshii looked crestfallen.

Paul smiled. "He saved our lives. He's one of the team now."

Toshii hugged the dog, receiving a face bath in return.

"What are you going to name him?" asked Daphne.

"Gojira." Toshii grinned.

Akiko school her head.

Paul made his way to the front of the boat. "Let's get out of here before any more—"

"Wait for me." The voice came from the river. Sparky swam toward them.

"Leave him," snapped Akiko. "The bastard left us."

Paul contemplated it but decided otherwise. He had not yet reached that level of inhumanity. Moving to the stern, Paul leaned out and offered his left hand, took Sparky's, and dragged him in. Halfway there, he paused, removed the Magnum, and placed the barrel between the kid's eyes.

"What the—"

"Shut up. I'm only going to say this once. You fuck us over again and I'll shoot you and leave you for the deaders. Understood?"

"Come on, man. I was—"

Paul cocked the hammer. "Understood?"

"I do. I do."

Paul lifted Sparky into the boat then shoved him onto the rear bench. "Sit there and shut up."

Akiko avoided eye contact with Paul as he made his way to the bow, fixing her gaze on Sparky, hatred filling her eyes.

Paul started the boat and continued down river. Daphne saddled up beside him.

"Would you really shoot him?"

"The kids an asshole and needs to be put in his place."

"But would you shoot him?"

Paul shook his head and smiled. He wouldn't shoot Sparky. At least, not yet.

Chapter Ten

PAUL GLANCED OVER his shoulder at Toshii. "Where did you learn to shoot like that?"

"Video games. I love first-person shooters."

Paul handed the controls to Daphne. Unholstering the Magnum, he loaded six bullets into the chamber and handed the revolver to Toshii.

The teenager's eyes widened. "You're giving this to me?"

"You did good back there, kid. You'll need it to protect you and your mother."

Toshii bowed. "*Domo arigato.*"

"Here." Paul removed the belt with the holster and handed it to Toshii. "You'll need this to store it."

"Don't I get a gun?" asked Sparky.

"You'll get a bullet if you don't shut up."

Paul returned to the bow and checked his denim jacket. The teeth marks from where the deader bit him dug deep into the material.

Daphne noticed and placed her hand on the Glock. "Were you bit?"

"We'll know soon enough." Paul slowly slid off the jacket, afraid of what he would find. The skin on his forearm was bruised but not broken. Paul rubbed his left hand along the wound and checked his fingers. No blood.

"I'm fine."

"Good." Daphne glanced over at him and smiled. "What now?"

"Pull over at the next wooded area so I can check the maps."

"Just so you know, those things can walk under water."

"Are you serious?"

Daphne nodded. "While I was waiting for you, forty deaders showed up on the opposite bank of the river. When they couldn't swim across, they walked. Next thing I knew, they were all around me."

"Shit. We can't underestimate them anymore." He thought for a moment. "Shut off the engine and let the current take us."

"Are we still heading to New Hampshire?"

"That's the plan. I'm going to check out the maps."

"Aye, aye, captain."

Paul sat down on the chair opposite her. He wanted to check on Alissa and see if she had survived. Picking up his jacket, he unzipped the inside pocket and removed his cellphone. The denim had absorbed most of the water, keeping the phone dry. He felt relieved when the screen lit up and the Apple logo appeared. Paul checked the power level, pissed that it had dropped below forty percent. Alissa had not responded to his earlier text message. He dialed her number, only to get the three-pitched tone followed by a recorded message stating all lines were busy. Three more attempts failed.

Shutting off the phone to conserve energy, he slipped it back inside his jacket. Paul removed the folded map from the backpack and spread it out on his lap. He ruled out continuing along the Monongahela River. It would only take them farther south away from New England. At some point, they would have to abandon the boat, commandeer a vehicle, and drive the rest of the way. He refused to take the I-95 corridor along the coast. Sure, it would take him straight into New Hampshire, but only after it passed through Washington, Baltimore, Philadelphia, and New York City. They would never make it through those hotspots. Time to look for a different route.

Twenty miles up ahead was Morgantown. From there, he

could follow one of the state roads paralleling I-66 to I-81, an interstate that ran north through agricultural country. He and Alissa had taken it once on a weekend trip to Gettysburg to avoid the traffic on I-95. For an interstate highway, it carried little traffic and bypassed major cities. Plus, there were enough secondary roads that they should be able to skirt around any hordes of deaders. Depending on their luck, they could be at the cabin in two days, three at most. Easy.

Paul laughed to himself. The chances of them making it to North Conway without problems were smaller than him winning Megabucks and dating Jennifer Aniston. At least he had a game plan and could adapt it as necessary. He remembered what his old man used to tell him.

Plan for best, prepare for the worst.

Chapter Eleven

P AUL STUFFED THE map into the pocket of the backpack then relayed his plan to Daphne. She agreed with it.

"I'm going to check with our passengers. Keep your eyes open for any abandoned vehicles we can use."

"Aye, aye, captain."

"You'd make a good pirate."

"Arrr, matey," Daphne responded in a horrible pirate imitation.

Paul went to the back. Akiko and Toshii sat on the port bench, the former hugging her son against her. Blood stained their hands, faces, and clothes, though truth be known none of them looked much better. Akiko appeared emotionally frail, which was natural considering she had watched her husband die twice and almost been killed along with her son. He hoped she would not crack from what she faced in the next few days. Toshii held it together much better than his mother. He scratched Gojira behind the ears. Despite his age, he had taken over as head of their household. It dawned on Paul that Akiko hugging Toshii was more for her sake than his.

Paul sat on the bench opposite them. "How are you two holding up?"

"As well as can be expected," answered Toshii.

"Good. Daphne and I are heading north to New Hampshire. I have a cabin in the mountains. It's well stocked with enough food, water, and ammunition to hold us for months. We plan to ride out the apocalypse there. You two are welcome to join us if you want."

"Thank you." Akiko bowed. "That is most kind of you. Are you sure we won't be a bother?"

"Of course not. I'm happy to have you."

"What about me?" Sparky sat sullenly on the stern bench.

"You're welcome, too, as long as you do as you're told." Akiko frowned.

"How will we get there?" asked Toshii.

"We're going to find a car and drive there."

"You mean steal a car?"

"We'll only take one that's been left behind."

Toshii approved. "Good."

"How did you wind up in Brownsville?"

Akiko lowered her head so Toshii answered for them.

"Dad had taken us on a vacation to see the States. We started in New York and Washington and were heading out west to see the Grand Canyon when the dead came back to life. We were lucky."

"How so?'

"We got bored with Washington and left a day early. If we hadn't, we'd be stuck in Washington right now."

"Is this happening everywhere?" asked Akiko.

Shit, he had never considered that this could be an isolated incident, though he doubted it. "I don't know. I'm assuming it is. The news said was that Pennsylvania was under martial law. We won't know for certain until we find a radio."

"We're also lucky we ran into someone like you," added Toshii.

Sparky muttered under his breath, "Little shit."

Paul cast Sparky a glare that immediately silenced him.

Akiko ignored the comment. "We had stopped for gas. Toshii and I were inside buying snacks when a man attacked my husband. At first we thought it was a fight until the man bit Isoroku."

"That's my father," said Toshii.

"Did anyone try to help him?" Paul glanced over at Sparky.

"I wasn't going to fuck with some madman. I tried calling 911 but the lines were busy."

"So, you left him out there?"

Sparky turned his head and focused on the river.

"The attacker severed one of Isoroku's arteries. He bled out within minutes then got up. When I called out to him, Isoruku and the original attacker came after us. We're lucky they didn't get inside or…."

"I'm sorry."

"It's not your fault. My husband would be honored to know that we met a man willing to put his life in danger to save us."

Sparky shifted uncomfortably in his seat.

Paul turned his attention to the asshole. "Hey Sparky, what about you?"

"My name is Clem."

"Do you have any family back in Brownsville?"

Sparky faced Paul. "Just my parents and little sister."

"Didn't you want to see if they're all right?"

Sparky shrugged. "They're probably dead by now."

"You aren't man enough to even check on your own family?" spat Akiko.

Sparky started to respond but stopped. He turned his attention back to the river.

"Don't worry," said Paul. "As long as you're with us, Daphne and I will take care of you."

Akiko bowed again. "Thank you."

"Paul," Daphne called out from the wheel. "Off to the left."

Up ahead was a clearing with a road beyond it. A police car sat at an angle across both lanes, its front doors open. Paul joined Daphne.

"Will that work?" she asked.

"It's too small. But pull over anyway."

"What for?"

"There might be weapons in it. With luck, I can find out

what's going on from the radio."

Daphne maneuvered the boat against the riverbank and stopped.

"If I don't make it back, proceed with the plan." Paul handed her his cellphone. "The address of the cabin and the codes to get in are all in here."

"What's your access code to the phone?"

"It's 6969."

Daphne cocked an eyebrow. "Seriously?"

"It's easy to remember." Paul grabbed the shotgun and crowbar and jumped onto the bank. "Sparky, you're with me."

"Why me?"

"Because you're expendable. Now move."

Sparky stood reluctantly and joined Paul. "I want a weapon."

Paul handed him the crowbar.

Sparky rolled his eyes. "Thanks."

The two men made their way to the car, Paul scanning the area for deaders. As they drew closer, Paul noticed bloody handprints on the doors but no bodies. Given what had been going on the past few hours, which did not surprise him. His concern was whether the deader had wandered off or lurked nearby. He raised the shotgun into the low-ready position.

When they reached the squad car, Sparky made his way to the open door and peered inside. "I call dibs on any weapons."

A deader in a hunter's outfit rose from the back seat and lunged at the kid, its teeth bared. With a feral growl, it clamped down, its teeth grinding together. Fortunately for Sparky, the deader bit the metal security gate between the front and back seats. Still, the kid screamed and jumped back, tripping against the open door and falling on his ass on the asphalt. Paul laughed.

"It's not funny," protested Sparky as he stood and attempted to salvage his dignity.

"Maybe now you learned a lesson. Check out an area before you go barging in."

Paul glanced into the back. The hunter deader had its hands cuffed behind its back, making it much less of a danger. Something had ripped a chunk of flesh out of the back of its neck and blood covered its shoulders. The deader turned to Paul and bit at the glass. He noticed bits of flesh and blood stains on its teeth. Whoever arrested him had more than likely been bitten and turned, but where was it now? With all the noise the hunter deader made, every deader in the area would be upon them in no time.

Paul slung the shotgun over his shoulder and held out his hand. "Let me have the crowbar."

"I'm not giving up my weapon."

"Fine by me." Paul placed his hand on the door handle. "I'll release it. You kill it."

Sparky handed the crowbar to Paul, who positioned himself three feet from the door. "Open it."

Sparky lifted the handle and pulled it open. The hunter deader scooted across the seat and began to climb out. With its head exposed, Paul raised the curved end of the crowbar and drove it into the back of the thing's skull, driving the metal in four inches. The deader convulsed then went limp, sliding off the weapon. Paul wiped off the blood on its clothes and handed it back to Sparky.

Blood smears covered the rear seat and security cage. Paul found nothing that could be useful. He checked out the front seat, including the glove compartment. Nothing. Reaching under the dashboard, he found the lever to unlock the trunk and pulled it.

"What are you doing?" asked Sparky.

"Hopefully, we'll find something useful in the trunk." Paul exited the squad car and lifted the trunk lid. "See."

A Mossberg shotgun with two spare boxes of shells, a riot helmet, a bullet-proof vest, a pair of two-way radios, and a medical kit lay inside. Paul took each of them out and handed them to Sparky.

"Take these back to the boat."

"Aren't you coming?"

"I want to see if I can reach someone on the radio."

As Sparky carried the newly acquired loot back to the boat, Paul slid into the front seat, picked up the microphone, and pressed the talk button.

"Is anyone out there?"

Silence.

Paul tried again.

This time a female voice came over the line. "Phil, is that you?"

"No, my name is Paul. Who's this?"

"Elaine. Which car are you calling from?"

"I don't know. I'm on a road running near the Monongahela River. I found it abandoned with a dead hunter in the back."

A moment of silence. "That's Phil's car. Is he there?"

"I don't see him. I think he was bit and wandered off."

"Oh, God." Elaine's voice cracked.

"What's the situation like out there?"

"Avoid Morgantown at all costs. Deaders have overrun the city. There are thousands of them in the streets. I'm the only one still alive."

"How are you holding out?"

"Not good. I'm stuck in the com center. There's a dozen of those things outside the door trying to get in."

"I'm trying to make it to New Hampshire. What's the situation up north?"

Elaine took a deep breath. "This outbreak occurred all over the world. Every major city and town are infected. Places like New York and Washington are death traps."

"What about Boston?" Paul thought about Alissa.

"The same. The entire east coast from Portsmouth to Miami has collapsed. Every state east of the Mississippi have declared martial law and imposed curfews. Your best bet is to head inland where there is little population."

"I have to get to New Hampshire."

"Then take the inland roads. Deader activity there is bad but the State Police reports the roads are passable."

"I'll do that. Hang on."

A deader in a police uniform ran down the road toward the squad car. Paul stepped out and unslung his shotgun. Using the door as a shield, he aimed. When the deader closed to within ten feet, he fired a single round that tore off its head. The deader somersaulted and landed on the asphalt. It still wore a holstered Glock. Paul undid the belt, which also included a taser and mace, and threw it over his shoulder. The officer's name tag read EASTMAN.

Paul returned to the squad car and picked up the microphone. "Sorry. The officer returned to his car. He had reanimated."

"Did you…?"

"Yes. His name was Eastman."

Elaine stifled a sob. "That was my fiancée. We were going to be married in April."

"Sorry. If it's any comfort, I put him out of his misery."

"Thank you."

"Do you want us to come and rescue you?"

"No. You'd only die trying. I appreciate it, though. I've resigned myself to my fate. I plan on taking my own life before those things can get to me."

"Good luck."

"You, too. And thank you for helping Phil. Signing off."

The radio went dead. Paul returned to the boat.

Sparky stood near the rear holding the shotgun over his shoulder. Daphne sat nervously by the wheel. Her eyes lit up on seeing him.

"We heard a gunshot. Are you okay?"

Paul nodded. "The officer had returned to the squad car.

He was a deader so I shot him."

Climbing into the boat, Paul offered the belt to Akiko. "Take this. You're the only one not armed."

Akiko backed into her seat and raised her hands. "No, thanks. I hate weapons."

"You have to defend yourself."

Akiko shook her head. Paul removed the taser and can of mace and handed them to her. "Take these, then. They should slow them down if you get trapped."

Reluctantly, she took the non-lethal weapons and placed them in her lap.

Paul handed the belt with the Glock to Sparky. "You take this and give the Mossberg to Daphne."

"No way, man. I'm not giving this up."

"Yes, you are."

"Come on, man. She can't handle a shotgun."

Daphne raced up from the bow. Though six inches shorter than Sparky, she got into his face.

"What are you trying to say?"

"N-nothing."

"You think because I'm a woman I can't defend myself?" Daphne refused to back down. "I'll have you know I've killed more deaders today than you have. And I'm not a coward."

"Hey. I'm not a coward."

"You are," Toshii said defiantly.

Even Akiko nodded in agreement.

Paul unslung his shotgun and aimed it at Sparky. "You can keep the Mossberg if you want, but you get off here."

Sparky knew when to back down. He handed the Mossberg and the two boxes of rounds to Daphne and wrapped the gun belt around his waist. As he sat down on the stern bench and looked out over the river, he mumbled, "Fuck you all."

Paul ignored him and returned to the controls with Daphne.

"You got spunk. I like that."

"I've been dealing with assholes like him all my life." Daphne sat in the passenger seat, the Mossberg between her legs. Her eyes fixed on Sparky. "Just because I'm small and have big tits doesn't mean I can be pushed around."

Paul smiled. Starting the engine, he pulled the boat away from shore and headed down river.

Chapter Twelve

T HE SUN INCHED its way toward the horizon, casting long shadows ahead on the boat. Paul had decelerated the engine, allowing the current to move the boat along, both the conserve fuel and to give him a chance to survey both banks for deaders, survivors, or any vehicle they could commandeer to get them to New Hampshire.

Daphne's eyelids became heavy. The crash following the adrenaline rush, the physical exertion of fighting deaders all day, and the gentle rocking of the boat lulled her. Without realizing it, her head fell back against the seat and she slowly slipped into a much-needed nap.

One thought occupied her mind. Paul. At first, she thought he was an asshole. Okay, she still thought he was an asshole, but a decent one. He nearly got himself killed saving her when he didn't have to. Shit, how many other people ran by without even giving her a notice? Paul didn't have to rescue her, didn't have to let her join him, didn't have to agree to allow her to join him in his cabin in New Hampshire. Without him, she would be a deader Happy Meal by now, or worse, one of the living dead. At first, she thought he'd pull one of these sex-for-safety deals. Granted, he was cute and kind of sexy when kicking ass, but no way would she put out like that. She had already proven her ability to take care of herself numerous times today.

Then Paul took in Akiko and Toshii. He even allowed that dickweed Sparky to come along. Daphne considered herself a good person, but even she would have left Sparky to drown or be eaten by deaders. Paul had street smarts, something she wished she had more of. He knew enough not to try and save large groups of people, realizing it would only get them all killed. Yet he had no qualms about risking his life to save Akiko and Toshii. Paul reminded her of the preppers on those reality shows she watched with her last boyfriend—knowledgeable, prepared, and not afraid to act yet devoid of that testosterone-laced pomposity the men on TV displayed. The more she got to know Paul, the safer she felt around him and the more she trusted him. He had a rough, prickly exterior but inside was sweet.

Daphne smiled. Paul was a coconut. That would be her nickname for him.

A minute later, she dozed off. She dreamed of the life she used to have before this morning. Of her small, one-bedroom, fifth floor apartment she rented on the outskirts of Pittsburgh. Of her job as a receptionist for a small law firm. Of the boyfriends she had since moving to the city after spending most of her life in Scranton. Three were extremely handsome but turned out to be macho dickheads. One cheated on her, even banging her best friend. The other two treated her like dirt. Her last boyfriend was Josh, a guy of average looks who treated her as a princess, but whose obsession with everything living dead made her break up with him a month ago. Right now, he must be having the time of his life or huddling in his apartment scared like a frightened kitten. After that, she could not recall anything.

A bright light shone in her face, rousing her from her slumber. It must be the sunrise.

Daphne covered her eyes. "You let me sleep all night?"

"You've only been asleep twenty minutes," answered Paul.

"Then where's the light coming from?"

"There."

Daphne opened her eyes. Ahead of them sat the town of

Griffin, ablaze.

An inferno covered the center of town, thick black smoke billowing into the night sky. Two tentacles of flames branched out from the center, one to the east extending to the McLellandtown Bridge, the other half a mile to the west reaching the riverbank. On the extent of land in between stood hundreds of people, trapped and waiting to be engulfed by the encroaching fire. More than a dozen had tried to swim to the other side, the current sweeping them away. A line of deader corpses stretched before the survivors. At least a few had guns, which made them potentially dangerous.

Paul stared at the shore, no emotion in his eyes.

Daphne clutched his hand. "You're not considering helping them, are you?"

"There's too many. It would cause a riot. We'd be lucky to make it out alive and, if we did, we'd be stuck there with the others."

Many of those on the bank noticed the boat, waving and shouting to catch their attention. Paul accelerated and swung toward the opposite bank. The calls for help turned to angry shouts. Some dived into the water and swam toward them, oblivious to the fact they could never catch the speeding boat. A few men fired shotguns at them.

"Everyone down." Paul crouched behind the wheel and zig-zagged to make a more difficult target. Daphne knelt beside him. Akiko wrapped her arms around Toshii and dragged him to the deck where Gojira joined them. In the back, Sparky hid behind the gunwale and returned fire into the crowd. They all fell onto the grass, including the shooters.

"Don't kill them," said Daphne.

"I'm shooting over their heads." Sparky turned his head and glared at her. "I stopped them firing at us, didn't I?"

Daphne switched her attention to Paul. He merely shook his head, in agreement with what the little shit had done. Paul kept his focus straight ahead.

"We're not in the clear yet."

Daphne stared down the river. Three uniformed figures stood in the center of the bridge, an overweight man and two teenage boys, waving at them. Paul pretended not to see them and accelerated to full throttle. The overweight man climbed over the railing and jumped. He hit the water one hundred feet in front of the boat with a heavy splash but never resurfaced. The two teenagers did the same. One misjudged, slamming into the piling beneath, leaving a red splotch of blood as his carcass careened into the river. The other landed thirty feet in front of the boat and reemerged. Paul steered right to avoid running him over.

The teenage boy reached up as the boat sped past and grabbed the gunwale with his left hand, being dragged along the surface.

Sparky jumped up and aimed the Glock at the teenager. "Let go or I'll blast you."

"Stop being a fucking ass." Daphne raced back and shoved Sparky aside, then reached out and grabbed the teenager's wrist. "Pull yourself in."

Due to the speed of the boat, he could not turn his body to grab the gunwale with his right hand.

"Paul, slow down."

Paul pulled the throttle back, allowing the boat to coast. The teenager grabbed the gunwale with his right hand. Toshii ran over to help and he and Daphne pulled the teenager into the boat. He fell onto the deck, panting as much from fear as exhaustion. Daphne noticed the uniform belonged to the Boy Scouts.

"Thanks." He coughed and spat up water. "I'm Ian."

"Daphne." She helped him to his feet. "This is Akiko and Toshii. The asshole who tried to shoot you is Sparky."

Sparky plopped into his seat and extended the middle finger.

"The guy driving the boat is Paul." Paul offered a half-

62

hearted wave.

The Boxer barked and wagged his tail.

"And that's Gojira."

"Hey, boy." Ian held out his hands. Gojira raced in for a pet.

"That was a dumb ass move jumping off the bridge," said Paul.

"We were desperate." Ian stood. "We had nowhere to go."

"What about heading home?" asked Akiko.

"Griffin is our home."

Akiko lowered her head. "I'm sorry."

"Don't be."

Paul shot a look over his shoulder. "What happened?"

"We had been camping and were on our way back to town when news came over the radio about the outbreak. Rusty... that was our troop leader. told the driver to head home so we could be with our loved one. About three miles out of town, a horde of those... things attacked us. Rusty, Ben, and I were the only ones to survive. We hiked back to town and found it on fire. One of the locals who escaped said some idiot was attacked at a gas station, fired his pistol, and blew up the station. I don't know if it's true. It'd explain the fire."

"You're welcome to stay with us, kid. Or I can drop you off here and you can make your way back to Griffin to check on your family."

"I'll stay with you, if you don't mind?"

"What about your family?"

"My mom divorced my dad and moved to Arizona with my little sister a year ago. My dad's a drunken bully. The only reason I'd go back is to shoot him in the head."

"If he had turned into a zombie?" asked Toshii.

"Of course." Ian grinned. "Where are you heading?"

"I have a cabin in northern New Hampshire. It's well-stocked and isolated. If we can get there, we can ride out this outbreak safely."

"That sounds great to me. I'll do whatever I can to help."

"Thanks, kid."

Ian sat down on the seat next to Toshii.

Daphne returned to the bow and kept watch as Paul headed down river.

Chapter Thirteen

"**T**HIS IS AS far as we go."

Paul stared at the obstacle blocking their path. So far, they had been lucky, but he knew that would not last. The trip down the Monongahela River had passed two sets of locks, one near Luzerne and the other to the south of Griffin. Fortunately, the operators had left the locks open so small craft could maneuver along the waterway. Their luck ran out outside of Atlantic. The rail bridge crossing the river had collapsed, or more likely been demolished, its span lying in the water. There was no way they could maneuver past it.

"What now?" Daphne moved closer.

"We passed a clearing earlier. We'll backtrack there and set out on foot."

"We're going to walk all the way to New Hampshire?" asked Akiko.

"Until we find an abandoned vehicle we can borrow."

Turning the boat around, Paul proceeded up the river until he spotted the clearing. The road sat at the top of a gentle hill. He pulled in alongside the river and throttled back the engine but left the motor running.

"Daphne, stay here. Sparky and I will check the road and make certain it's clear. If something happens to us, haul ass out of here. Okay?"

"I'm not leaving you."

"If this goes south, you won't have a choice." He patted Daphne on the arm. "I'm relying on you."

Daphne forced a smile.

Paul made his way to the rear of the boat and jumped over the side. "Sparky, you're with me."

"Why me?"

"Because I don't trust you. I want to keep an eye on you."

Daphne cleared her throat. She held the Mossberg in both hands. Sparky got the message and joined Paul. Their weapons raised into the low-ready position, both men inched their way up to the road.

Paul stood in the center and scanned both directions. He could not see far because of the moonless night, but he detected no signs of movement. Raising his Mossberg into the high-ready position, he whistled loudly.

"Are you out of your fucking mind? You'll call those things down on us."

"Better to know now if there are deaders in the area rather than a mile down the road."

Except for the hum of the boat's engine, silence enveloped the area.

Paul whistled a second time.

A twig snapped in the woods thirty yards to their right. Both men spun in the direction of the noise and aimed, waiting to rain down a barrage of gunfire on the living dead. Another twig snapped, followed by the rustling of branches. They waited. Sweat collected on Paul's brow. Sparky's hands shook.

The bushes between two trees separated and a deer emerged onto the asphalt. It paused to stare at the humans and, not detecting a threat, sauntered over to the other side and disappeared into the woods.

Sparky exhaled. "Why did the deer cross the road?"

"Why?"

"To scare the fucking shit out of us."

Despite himself, Paul laughed. "Let's get the others."

Lowering their weapons, both men returned to the boat.

Akiko seemed concerned. "Is everything okay?"

"We saw a deer. That's all." Paul climbed in and moved to the bow, removing the map from the dashboard. He studied it.

Daphne stepped up beside him. "What are you doing?"

"Getting our bearings. I don't want to wander into a town and be overrun."

"Should we wait until morning?"

Paul shook his head. "I want to get far away from here as soon as possible. There's too much deader activity along the river. Point Marion is ahead of us. There's a road before it that leads away from the area. Route 119. We'll take that and head inland. With luck, we'll find a car by dawn." He folded the map and handed it to Daphne. "I want you and Ian to bring up the rear and watch our six for anything following us."

"What about asshole?"

"He's with me so I can keep an eye on him. I don't fully trust him yet. Is that okay?"

Daphne snapped to attention and saluted, a grin piercing her lips. Paul could not help but notice how her chest bounced.

"Aye, aye, captain."

Paul sighed and stepped over to Ian, withdrawing his Glock. "Kid, have you ever used a weapon before?"

"I went hunting with my dad a few times."

"Good enough." Paul handed Ian the Glock. The kid slid the weapon between his back and the rear of his pants. He did not seem intimidated by it, which was good. "The safety is in the trigger. Don't point it anything you don't want to kill."

"Yes, sir."

"Don't call me sir, I'm Paul."

"Roger that."

Paul faced the others. "We're going to walk from here. Sparky and I will take the lead and Daphne and Ian will bring up the rear. Grab all the gear you can. If we're attacked, it's every man for himself. Any questions?"

"What about the boat?" asked Daphne.

"Leave the keys in it. We take only what we need and leave

the rest for others. Let's move out."

Five minutes later, the party was on the road heading east toward Route 119.

THE GROUP WALKED through the night and for an hour after sunrise. They took ten-minute breaks every hour, though no one relaxed. No one talked, worried that any noise would attract deaders. Even Gojira remained quiet, not barking once. Everyone knew they were in the middle of an apocalypse and that, with each passing minute, the number of living dead increased. At any moment, a nightmarish death could descend on them. Route 119 was isolated so they passed few populated areas, and those were empty. The only saving grace was that the farther they walked the more confident they became of a slight chance of making it out alive.

Emphasis on the word slight.

"My feet are killing me," Daphne protested to herself.

Ian kept his eyes to the right, scanning for danger. "Flats were made for comfort, not for hiking."

"I didn't know I'd be running for my life when I left for work this morning." Daphne paused. "Sorry if that sounded snippy."

"It didn't. Besides, judging by the looks of you, you've been through a lot today."

"What do you mean?"

"All the blood."

Daphne pulled out the bottom of her sweater and stared. For the first time, she noticed that dried blood stained the front of it. When she let the sweater fall back into place, she saw blood stains on the legs of her jeans.

"Don't worry about it," said Ian. "We're all covered in blood. You and Paul more than others."

"I look horrid."

"You look great." Ian spun around to face Daphne, his cheeks turning fifty shades of red. "I meant you don't look horrible. But you do look good. Covered in blood."

"I know what you meant." She gently touched Ian's upper arm, producing more shades of red. "And thank you."

Ian turned his attention back to the woods trying to hide his embarrassment.

TEN MINUTES LATER, Paul stopped the group.

Akiko moved beside him. "Is everything okay?"

"We may have found our way out of here."

A quarter of a mile ahead of them, a Dodge Ram that had seen better days sat along the side of the road. The fire engine red paint had lost its shine and rust formed around the wheel wells, running boards, and the edges of the rear gate. A grime-covered topper rested on top of the bed.

"Stay here while we check it out."

Paul and Sparky approached the pick-up from the left and right, respectively. Sparky stepped up to the topper and knocked on the Plexiglas door. When no noise came from the back, he lifted the lid.

"Holy shit."

Paul moved alongside him. "Bad?"

"No. We hit the fucking jackpot."

A sleeping bag sat rolled up on the right side of the bed. To the left sat a wooden crate filled with canned goods and water and an open duffel bag containing a .233 caliber hunting rifle, a snub-nosed .38 caliber revolver, a government-issued Colt 1911 semi-automatic pistol, and a .357 magnum along with scores of boxes of ammunition for each weapon.

Sparky reached in and withdrew the rifle. "Who would be stupid enough to leave this behind?"

"The better question is why did they leave it behind. Let's

check the cab."

Both men separated and made their way to the front of the Ram. Tinted windows on the driver and passenger doors prevented them from seeing inside. Paul knocked on the window. Nothing. He opened the door and jumped back, aiming his Vepr at the cab. It was empty. Paul searched the compartment.

"Whoever left did so in a hurry. The keys are still in the ignition."

"I know why they abandoned it. The right front tire is flat." Sparky came around to Paul's side, still holding the hunting rifle. "I can change it out with the spare in a few minutes."

"I assume you want the rifle."

"Fuck yeah."

"It's yours. Grab the extra ammo from the back."

Paul waved for the others to join him. As they did, he went back to the bed and checked the Magnum. It was loaded. He slid it into the rear of his pants and tossed the extra ammo into his backpack. He handed the Colt 1911 and three spare magazines to Ian.

"Thanks. Does it run?"

"Let me check before I waste my time changing the flat." Sparky climbed into the driver's seat and turned the key. The engine roared to life. He shut it off and crawled out. "Let me get to work on that tire."

Paul called Daphne over. "There's a .38 in back with several boxes of ammo. It's yours. There's also a box of supplies. Do you mind taking inventory?"

"Of course." Daphne lowered the gate, climbed in back, and slid the revolver under her sweater against her back. She tossed the boxes of ammo into her backpack then pulled the crate of food closer to her.

Sparky dropped to the ground and ass-walked under the chassis. "Fuck."

"What's wrong?"

"There's no spare." Sparky came out and stood. "That explains why they didn't change it."

Gojira moved closer to Toshii and growled.

"What's wrong, boy?"

The dog stared down the road and barked three times.

"Shut that dog up," snapped Sparky.

Paul raised his Vepr into the high-ready position and scanned the area.

A rustling came from the woods.

"Get in the cab," ordered Paul.

Sparky turned to him. "We all won't fit."

"You and I are on the roof."

Sparky scrambled up the hood. Ian jumped in the cab first and scooted over to the passenger side, followed by Toshii and Akiko. Paul helped Gojira climb in then slammed the door. The dog barked furiously.

"Lock it and stay inside no matter what."

As Paul circled around to the hood, a deader in hunting clothes emerged from the woods. Paul aimed the Vepr and fired. The round struck the hunter deader in the face. The body collapsed onto the asphalt.

Paul reached the roof as over a hundred deaders swarmed from the woods and surrounded the Ram.

Chapter Fourteen

DAPHNE WAS HALF-WAY out of the bed when the horde broke through the tree line. Realizing she had no chance in the open, she rolled back in and slammed shut the tailgate. Thirteen deaders centered themselves in the gap provided by the open hatch, reaching for her. Daphne crawled to the front of the truck, leaving the Mossberg by the tailgate.

Removing the .38 from under her sweater, she aimed at the head of the center deader and squeezed the trigger.

IAN FELT HELPLESS as the deaders smashed against the passenger window and flowed around the Ram, surrounding the pick-up. Two deaders stared at him through the side window, one a female EMT with its face chewed off, the other an older man with no right arm that still wore the blue vest of a Walmart employee, the cloth drenched in blood. They bit and clawed at the glass, leaving trails of smudged blood along the surface.

Others moved around the fenders and made their way to the driver's side, desperate to get in. Akiko screamed and hugged Toshii tight. Gojira jumped in her lap and placed its front paws on the window, barking at the deaders.

Ian held the Colt Paul had given him. Withdrawing it, he studied the situation. He did not have enough rounds to take care of them all but, if any broke through the glass, he would make certain they would have to work hard for their meal.

Two deaders jumped onto the hood. A male with no shirt and half its chest eaten away slammed its head against the windshield, sending a spider web crack along the surface. The other, in a fire fighter's uniform, bounded up onto the roof.

DOZENS OF DEAD arms reached across the topper, forcing the two men to stand side by side. The stench of decomposition was nauseating, far worse than in Pittsburgh. And with the bodies beginning to decay, swarms of flies and wasps covered them, feeding off the rotting flesh. The buzz they generated was overwhelming.

"Behind you."

Sparky stepped to Paul's side and fired at the firefighter deader. The bullet knocked the helmet off its head. It paused, stunned by the blast. He fired again, this time catching it between the eyes, splattering blood and brains across the hood and sending a mass of insects airborne, many of which went after them. The deader toppled over and rolled onto the road.

Paul shouldered his shotgun and removed his Magnum. Aiming it at the closest deader, he fired. Its head erupted, disturbing another mass of bugs. Paul waved his hand in front of his face to brush them away, ignoring the angry wasps that stung him. As the deader fell to the side of the pick-up, another rushed into its place. Paul lined up his shot and took it down. With each deader eliminated, more flies and wasps took to flight, swarming around their faces and making it difficult to aim.

DAPHNE CONTINUED FIRING until the .38 was empty. Reaching into her backpack, she removed six rounds and quickly reloaded. Flies, wasps, and putrid chunks of dead flesh filled the rear of the deck. This must be what Hell is like.

She finished reloading. A deader in farmer's overalls, its

beard covered in blood and gore, crawled into the back. It would have attacked but its bulky stomach caught in the opening. She double tapped it in the head, putting the creature out of its misery. The good news was that the body blocked the others from getting in, but it also prevented her from escaping.

THE SHIRTLESS DEADER continued to smash its head against the windshield, leaving blood smears across the glass. On the fifth strike, the windshield fractured. The deader stuck its head in, widening the crack as the glass grated the skin off its face. It focused on Toshii, snarled, and pushed its way toward him.

Ian swung the Colt in its direction. The glass beside him shattered. The EMT and Walmart deaders reached in, grabbed his arm, and pulled it toward their hungry mouths.

At the same moment, the driver's window caved in, showering Akiko with glass shards. A deader in a National Guard uniform reached in, its hands wildly grasping at the woman. Akiko shrieked.

PAUL HEARD THE shattering of glass and Akiko's scream. He turned and fired a round into the National Guard deader, blasting a hole in its back and shattering its shoulder blades. It pulled out of the cab, looked up at him, and opened its mouth. Paul blasted off its head. As it fell, another deader in a Pennsylvania State Police uniform rushed into its spot.

Sparky finished reloading his hunting rifle and noticed the shirtless deader on the hood, its head buried through the windshield. He fired at its back. The bullet struck but did insignificant damage. He shot off three more rounds. Its legs went limp but its arms still worked. Shoving them through the windshield, it dragged itself inside.

Sparky heard the passenger window shatter and shifted his attention to that side of the Ram, pumping round after round into the deaders but unable to get a head shot. They continued to attack those in the cab.

A FRENZIED FEMALE deader in a torn Dunkin Donuts shirt and visor, a chunk of human flesh hanging off the latter, pushed its way past the fat deader's corpse on the left as a deader in a gore-stained construction worker's vest crawled in on the right. Daphne aimed the .38 at the former's forehead. It hissed at Daphne, spitting bloody saliva at her.

"Fuck you, bitch!" Daphne pulled the trigger.

Click.

Fuck.

Daphne slammed her left leg into the face of the Dunkin Donuts deader, hoping to knock it onto the road. It moved back a foot then stopped, its right hand clasped around the fat deader's belt. Daphne kicked it in the face three more times, fracturing its jaw and dislodging three teeth, but the thing would not relent. Placing her left foot against its face, Daphne leaned back and reached for her backpack.

The construction deader had climbed a third of the way into the bed before its vest became entangled in the lid's hinges. It flailed around, trying to get free. One half-chewed hand reached in for a hold, its decayed fingers wrapping around the strap to Daphne's backpack and pulling it close. Daphne grabbed the bottom and yanked, engaging in a tug of war with it as a Dunkin Donuts deader clawed her leg and gnawed at her flats. The struggle ended when the construction deader's vest tore. The deader fell into the bed face-first, releasing the backpack.

Daphne pulled it toward her and reached inside. The jostling had disturbed the contents. Frantic, she felt around for the box of ammo.

The construction deader raised itself on its elbows.

The Dunkin Donuts deader grabbed bit into Daphne's flat.

Daphne's found the open box of ammo and pulled it out. The bullets spilled out across the floor of the deck.

Its milky eyes focusing on her, the construction deader snarled and crawled across the bed.

The Dunkin Donuts deader dragged itself up Daphne's leg.

Daphne loaded a single bullet into the revolver. The construction deader's jaw was inches from her face. Reaching out, she slammed the palm of her left hand against its chin, preventing it from biting her. Its mouth frantically snapped at her fingers.

The Dunkin Donuts deader still gnawed at Daphne's shoe.

God, don't let me die this way.

Daphne laid the revolver on the metal deck and, with her right hand, picked up a bullet, slid it into an empty chamber, and closed it. Grabbing the revolver, she placed the barrel on the construction deader's temple and fired.

Click.

Click.

Click.

The sound was deafening when the hammer struck the bullet. The top of the deader's head disintegrated. It fell on top of Daphne's chest. She pushed it aside.

The Dunkin Donuts deader tore at her foot like a dog chewing on a bone. Daphne rolled to her left, raised her right leg, and kicked, catching the deader in the forehead. She repeated the move twice until it released its grip. Daphne pulled herself into the bed, quickly loaded the chamber, and fired. The first bullet entered its right eye, killing it. The rest of the rounds ripped apart dead flesh.

The Dunkin Donuts deader's corpse slid out of the opening. Another one took its place.

Daphne slipped off her flat to check her foot, sighing in relief when she saw that the deader had not bitten through her shoe.

IAN SHIFTED THE Colt to his left hand and double tapped each deader. The EMT deader slipped out the window. The Walmart deader slumped forward into Ian's lap. He ignored it. Switching the weapon to his right hand, he shifted in his seat to shoot the shirtless deader coming through the windshield.

Gojira blocked his aim. Sensing Toshii was in danger, the dog had jumped in the boy's lap, barking and snapping at the deader. It reached out for Toshii. Gojira bit down on the deader's wrist and thrashed his head from side to side. All the dog succeeded in doing was pulling the thing farther into the cab.

Akiko reached her hand out to Ian. "Give me the gun."

Ian did. Akiko placed it against the shirtless deader's head and fired three times. The third bullet shattered its head, covering those inside the cab with gore. Toshii was safe… for now. Akiko then took down the State Police deader.

More flocked to get at them.

THE PILE OF bodies around the Ram gave the remaining deaders a foothold, allowing them to get closer to Paul and Sparky. Clutching hands reached out at them from all sides, forcing the two to jump around to prevent being pulled overboard.

A deader in a coveralls clutched Sparky's left leg. He slammed his other foot down on its arm, shattering the wrist. As its grip loosened, he kicked it back into the horde.

"We've barely killed half of them." Sparky reloaded. "Maybe we should make a break for it."

"We won't get far. And what about the others?"

"If we run, it might lead the horde away." Sparky killed another one. "It's better than dying up here."

Paul contemplated the idea when the blare of a car horn sounded behind them. They all turned at the noise.

A green Chevy Suburban raced down the road. It increased

speed as it drew closer and swerved in their direction. For a moment, Paul thought it would rear end them. At the last second, the driver turned, aiming for the horde along the left side of the Ram.

"Hang on."

The Suburban slammed into the deaders, bouncing over the bodies and ripping away those swarming against the pickup, crushing and smearing them along the side. The rest were either run over by the Suburban or bounced across the road. It continued ahead with most of the surviving deaders giving chase.

Paul lowered the Mossberg at a deader watching the vehicle speed past and fired. "Let's move while we have the chance."

The two men quickly cleared the last remaining deaders from around the Ram. Paul descended first, using the hood as a stair and being careful not to trip over the body of the shirtless deader stuck in the windshield or slip on the gore. He broke right and checked the side of the Ram. Sparky did the same on the left.

Gojira barked.

Paul moved closer to the window. "Was anyone bitten?"

"No," answered Ian.

"Sparky, get them out. I'll check on Daphne."

As he made his way to the back of the Ram, a screeching of brakes caught his attention. The Suburban had stopped a quarter of a mile down the road, allowing the deaders to catch up. They covered the vehicle.

"What the fuck are they doing?" asked Sparky.

"Keep an eye on them. We don't need any more trouble."

DAPHNE NOTICED THE Suburban a moment before it swept past them, tearing away the deaders. Shock turned to relief when those trying to get at her ran off after the vehicle.

She loaded the empty chambers, gathered up the stray bullets, and tossed them in her backpack. She scooted toward the tailgate when Paul centered himself in the opening. He grinned upon seeing her.

"Are you okay?"

"I've had better days." She pointed to the fat deader. "Help me get him loose so I can get out of here."

Paul grabbed its legs and pulled but the deader was wedged between the tailgate and the topper. He reached under, found the latch, and yanked. The tailgate fell open, dropping the deader onto the asphalt. Daphne slid out and hugged Paul.

"I'm glad you're okay."

"Same here." When Paul hugged her back, her arms tightened around him. Then she broke the hold. "What happened?"

"Somebody in a Suburban cleared out the deaders and led the others away."

"I wish I could thank him."

"You might get your chance." Sparky walked up to the others and pointed toward the Suburban.

Its back-up lights had come on. The Suburban reversed through the swarm, slowly at first, then rapidly increasing speed as it approached. Paul's group readied their weapons, not knowing what to expect. When fifty feet away, the passenger window rolled down. A lady in her mid-fifties stuck her head out.

"Get in. And hurry."

No one had to be told twice. The deaders ran toward them.

Sparky helped Toshii and Akiko into the third row of seats, then jumped in with them. Gojira launched himself in back, cuddling up against Toshii's legs. Ian got in next.

"You first," ordered Paul.

"I'll be back." Daphne ran to the rear of the Ram as Paul called after her.

Reaching into the bed of the Ram, she pulled the crate of

food toward her and lifted. It weighed more than expected but she could still lift it. Rushing back to the Suburban, she handed the crate to Paul who passed it to Ian.

The closest deader, a young girl wearing a ripped and soiled Catholic School uniform, was twenty feet away.

Daphne jumped in beside Paul, closing the door behind her. The deader ripped the door out of her hands and centered itself in the opening. Paul pushed Daphne against the seat, extended his left arm, and blasted the deader with his Mossberg.

The driver accelerated quickly, the forward motion forcing the door shut. As the Suburban barreled down the road, Daphne turned around to glance out back. The deaders, though still giving chase, were falling far behind them.

Chapter Fifteen

"**W**HAT THE HELL were you thinking?" snapped Paul.

Daphne reached across him and tapped the crate on Ian's lap. "I couldn't leave this behind. God knows when we'll find supplies again."

Paul stared at her, more admiration and fear than anger in his eyes.

The middle-aged lady from the front seat shifted so she could look at them. Her shoulder-length hair was tinged white and gray. Wrinkles covered her face, more from hard work than a hard life. Of average height and build, she wore jeans, a white denim shirt, and work boots. The woman had a pleasant demeanor about her.

"I give the young lady credit. She's got balls. She'll need them to survive out here."

"Thanks." Daphne gently nudged Paul in the side.

"Is everyone okay? I assume no bites."

"Just from wasps," said Paul. "I have three or four."

"Me, too." Sparky felt his face. "One bit me in the cheek. It hurts like a son of a bitch."

"Wimps," chided Daphne. "I got at least six stuck in the bed."

"We've always been tougher than men. You don't see them giving birth." The woman extended her hand. "Rebecca Daniels. But everyone calls me Becca."

"I'm Paul." He shook Becca's hand. "This is Daphne and Ian. In back is Sparky, Akiko, and Toshii."

The dog barked.

"Sorry, and Gojira."

"The boy must have named him," said the driver. "All kids his age love Godzilla. At least my three sons and grandkids did. I watched every *kaiju* movie they could find at least three times."

"I like him," Toshii whispered to his mother.

"Thank God you came along when you did otherwise we'd be part of that horde."

"Thank Becca here." The driver nodded in the woman's direction. "She got a flat tire trying to get out of the area and walked back to my place to ask my help in changing it."

"You would have been out of luck," Sparky said from the back. "There wasn't a spare."

"Becca." The driver shook his head good-naturedly.

"Sorry. I had other things on my mind."

The driver glanced into the rearview mirror. A robust man in his late fifties, he dressed conservatively in jeans and work boots but with a red flannel shirt. His hair and beard were solid white. He had piercing blue eyes that hinted at a friendliness tinted with hardness. He reminded Paul of Ernest Hemingway.

"I'm Ed, by the way. Ed Ketteridge. I used to live a few miles from here."

"Used to?" asked Daphne.

"No sane person would stick around. Too many of them flesh eaters. All the towns along the river have been infected, and the news says Pittsburgh was overrun and those things are heading south."

Daphne looked over at Paul. "We got out just in time."

"You were in Pittsburgh?" asked Becca.

Paul spent the next ten minutes relating what happened to him and Daphne and how they had met the others. When finished, Becca shook her head.

"God was with you all."

"God had nothing to do with it." Sparky sneered. "We

fought our way out."

"A lot of people fought," responded Becca. "Most didn't make it. I still maintain we survived thanks to God's good grace."

Sparky wanted to reply, but the glare he received from Paul warned him to keep his mouth shut.

Ed swerved to avoid a squirrel crossing the road. "Where are you headed?"

"New Hampshire."

"What's in New Hampshire?"

"I have a cabin in the mountains. It's isolated, well-stocked, and has plenty of guns and ammo."

"You a survivalist?"

"Amateur prepper. I always thought there would be civil unrest or an economic collapse someday and wanted a safe haven to go to." Paul chuckled. "I never imagined the dead would come back to life."

"No one did."

"You're welcome to join us."

Ed glanced over at Becca. "What do you think?"

"They don't want some old fogeys like us tagging along."

"You're far from old fogeys," Paul answered with a smile. "Besides, I think the two of you know a lot we can learn from you."

Ed laughed. "A smart millennial. Who would ever have thought?"

Becca rolled her eyes. "Ignore him. He's an old coot."

"New Hampshire it is then." Ed grinned. "Settle back and relax, folks. It's going to be a long ride."

Chapter Sixteen

ED KNEW THE backroads of Pennsylvania as well as he knew the back of his hand, which allowed him to avoid populated areas as they made their way east to I-81. He switched from one back road to another and passed through state parks and forests. After driving for more than three hours, they crossed the Susquehanna River near Duncannon, a few miles north of Harrisburg, and traveled cross country paralleling the Appalachian Mountains. The apocalypse had not extended this far into the countryside, at least not yet. They passed a handful of vehicles heading in the opposite direction but saw no abandoned cars, dead bodies, or signs of violence. And best of all, no deaders.

Becca fiddled with the radio in the hopes of getting updated information on the local situation, which proved difficult. All Pittsburgh stations had gone off the air early that morning and, between the distance and the mountains, the sole remaining radio station in Philadelphia came in spotty at best. SiriusXM cancelled its entertainment programming, running their CNN newscast on all non-news channels. The coverage was global, which did not help them much. In fact, listening to the casts was depressing. Deaders had swarmed through every major city around the globe, causing many of them to lose contact with the outside world. Every country with an open press reported similar outbreaks in major cities and towns, with the symptoms being identical. Even those countries like Iran and North Korea that maintained tight control over their media could not prevent rumors of the outbreak from reaching the west through the Internet and cell phones. Like their American counterparts, no one could identify what caused this pandemic. Interspersed between the news were interviews with "experts" who blamed the outbreak on everything from climate change, the decline of Christianity, and even one moron who claimed the deader virus was a permutation of COVID-19.

Once the stories repeated themselves, Becca switched over to FOX. A female correspondent read reports from around the world, all of them the same. The world was falling apart around them. You could detect the fear and frustration in her voice. Halfway through one update on the Prime Minister of England being killed when 10 Downing Street was overrun, she paused before resuming.

This just came in from Reuters. It's from the President of the United States. I'm reading directly from the communique. As of noon today, Eastern Standard Time, 0900 Pacific Time, a state of martial law will be declared across the country. All citizens are ordered to either shelter in place until the crisis is over or make their way to a local military installation or designated safe haven. Anyone caught outside after noon today will be detained and quarantined. This measure is being taken to stop the spread of the infection and give local police and the National Guard time to contain the situation.

Ed huffed. "Good luck enforcing that."

"What time is it?" asked Daphne.

Becca checked her watch. "It's 11:45."

"Nothing like giving everyone plenty of time." Paul leaned closer. "Shouldn't we have reached I-81 by now?"

"If we headed there directly, yes. But that would have meant going through Harrisburg, which is probably a nightmare." Ed patted the map spread out beside him. "I know of an exit that has only a few gas stations and fast-food restaurants. There should be fewer deaders there. We'll be there soon."

Paul sat back, wishing he were the one driving. He trusted

Ed but hated the idea of not being in control of the situation.

Ten minutes later, the Suburban approached the outskirts of Bethel. Ed announced, "Here we are."

Ahead of them sat a gas station/truck stop off to the right and a MacDonald's across the street. Two semi-trailers blocked the road. One had pulled out of the gas station too quickly, more than likely escaping deaders, and the rig tore through and became lodged in the opposite trailer. Half a dozen deaders milled around the body of the second driver who they had ripped from his cab, feasting on his remains. Seven more wandered along this side of the road.

"We're blocked," said Becca.

Ed grinned. "I can easily go around that."

At the sound of the engine, the deaders turned in their direction, snarled, and rushed the Suburban.

Ed accelerated. Paul, Daphne, and Sparky readied their weapons.

Swerving the steering wheel gently to the left and ring, Ed crashed through the pack. Most slammed off the sides of the Suburban and fell to the side of the road. One got under the front tire. The Suburban swung from side to side as the right wheels drove over it. Ed kept on going and maneuvered around the rear of the trailer into the gas station.

Becca gasped.

The Suburban crashed through a wave of thirty deaders that had been milling around the gas pumps. Ed ignored them, checking out the station. As he feared, close to two dozen cars filled the spaces between and behind the pumps. There was no clear space. Swerving right, he headed for the rear of the station, hoping to go around it. The surviving deaders gave chase. Ed turned the corner, nearly rear ending a parked Coca-Cola truck that had been supplying the store, then steered around the opposite side of the building.

A Toyota Ram-4 blocked their path. The driver's door was open, a deader in a MacDonald's uniform feeding off the driver. Ed did not have time to go around the carnage so he sped up, slamming into the deader and the open door, sending both careening across the asphalt. He continued without pausing, swinging the Suburban onto the road leading to the on-ramp to I-81 North.

A National Guard Humvee approached the on-ramp from the east traveling at close to eighty miles an hour. It swerved onto the ramp but, because of the angle of the turn and the speed, rolled onto its side and bounced down the road toward the Suburban, coming to a stop fifty feet away. Ed veered right and hugged the guardrail. The space between the Humvee and guardrail was narrow. Ed lowered his speed and raced through, tearing of the driver's side mirror. Slowing even further, he turned onto the ramp and gunned the engine, racing to safety.

Paul turned to look out the back.

Two Guardsmen crawled on the exposed side of the Humvee, only to be set upon by the deaders. One had his leg pulled out from under him and fell to the ground where a pack of deaders ravaged him. The second fired her Carbine at the pack, taking out five. She reloaded, jumped down by the undercarriage, and limped away. She made it only three yards before the remaining deaders rounded the front fender and took her down.

Paul shifted forward and patted Ed on the shoulder. "Good job back there."

"Thanks. Let's hope we can make a few hundred miles before we run into any more of those things."

A FEW EXITS to the north, a Pennsylvania State Police squad car sat sideways across then highway, blocking the left lane, its blue lights flashing. Nothing interfered with the right lane. It was an exit that led to back roads rather than cities or towns. The only sign of civilization was a large Exxon sign that hovered above the trees plus scores of bodies spread around the area, a mixture of deaders and State Troopers. A single trooper exited the driver's side of the squad car and walked around to the left fender. He held a Mossberg with the barrel pointing down.

"What time is it?" asked Ed.

Becca checked her watch. "A little after one."

Ian placed the Colt between his knees, grasping the grip and his index finger on the trigger guard.

The trooper waved them down.

Ed rolled down his window and stopped.

"Afternoon, officer."

"Where are you all heading?" the trooper asked. His breastplate bore the name NOWACK.

"North. We're trying to reach New Hampshire."

"You'll never make it on this route. I-81 is swarming with deaders between Wilkes-Barre and Scranton. Last report stated their heading south. I'm warning people not to stay on the highway."

Becca leaned to the side. "You're not going to arrest us for breaking curfew?"

"No one around here is enforcing that. We're just trying to survive." Nowack paused. "Did you say you were heading to New Hampshire?"

Ed motioned in back to Paul. "He has a cabin in the mountains. We're going to ride this out there."

"I wouldn't recommend it. New Hampshire and Vermont closed off their borders to anyone coming from the south. There are thousands of those things massing along the state lines. Even if you made it that far, you'd die attempting to get through."

"What about the I-95 corridor?" asked Paul.

"It's a death trap. Every major city between Boston and Miami has fallen. Deaders are spreading north and south."

Daphne clasped his hand. "What do we do now?"

Paul thought about it. "Our best bet is to get to the coast. We can find a boat that'll take us to Maine and steal a car from there."

Akiko shook her head. "The coast is a long way off."

"At least we know what's waiting for us in New Hampshire. Everything else is a crap shoot. Who's in?"

Everyone but Akiko and Sparky raised their hand.

"It's settled. The coast it is." Ed focused his attention on Nowack. "What about you?"

Nowack shook his head. "I'll stay here until the deaders get close then head inland, find a cabin to shack up in, and hope for the best. I suggest you do the same, but it's your choice."

"We'll take our chances. Thanks."

"Good luck." Nowack waved and headed back to his squad car.

Ed backed up the Suburban then took the off ramp to Route 125. "Here goes nothing."

Chapter Seventeen

J UST BEFORE TURNING onto Route 125, Ed pulled into the Exxon Station and stopped in front of the pumps. As he turned off the ignition, he turned to those in back.

"Might as well fill up now while we can. Besides, this place looks safe."

"I'll go in and switch on the pumps for you." Sparky patted Paul on the shoulder. "Can you let me out?"

Paul opened the door and stepped out, keeping his Mossberg ready in case danger showed up.

Sparky jumped out and headed for the entrance. The door was locked. He used the stock of his hunting rifle to shatter the glass, reached in to unlock the door, and entered. A minute later he rapped on the window and gave a thumbs-up. Ed had already placed the nozzle in the tank. Selecting the highest grade, he pressed the lever. The pump began chugging.

Gojira whimpered and danced around the back. The dog jumped out, ran to the grassy section out front, and squatted.

Akiko joined Paul. "That's a good idea. I'm going to see if Sparky has the keys to the restroom."

"I wouldn't risk going in there. God knows what might be waiting for you. I'd do it out here."

Akiko looked appalled.

Daphne joined them. "I have to go, too. We'll do it around back where no one will see us. Becca, you want to join us?"

"Sure." She opened the door and stepped back. "Better than peeing my pants."

"Be careful," warned Paul.

"I will." Daphne answered like a frustrated teenager. She tapped the Mossberg on her shoulder. "I have Black Widow."

"Black Widow?"

"You know. Scarlett Johansen plays her in the movies. Beautiful and deadly." Daphne winked. "Like me."

Ed chuckled. "She's a keeper."

Paul rolled his eyes.

When the women disappeared behind the station, Ed stepped over to a garbage bin and unzipped his fly.

"What are you doing?"

"The same thing the women are." A stream of urine drenched the bin.

Paul did the same, relieving himself on the cement.

Toshii joined him. "This is fun. My mother always takes me into the ladies' room with her."

When they finished, Gojira raced over, sniffed the wet spots, and marked the territory as his own.

Sparky exited the store carrying six heavy bags that he placed in the back.

"What are those?" asked Paul.

"I emptied the store of the remaining bottles of water and energy drinks. I figured we'd need them. I also switched on all the pumps in case someone has to fill up."

"Good thinking."

Ed came around and removed a bottle from one of the bags. "Where there any plastic gas cans in there?"

Sparky nodded. "I saw six of them by the counter."

"We should take advantage of this while we can. Come on."

Paul followed Ed inside and helped him carry out the containers. Using a second pump, Ed filled each one, which Paul sealed and placed in the back deck. The women returned before they finished.

"What now?" asked Becca.

"We'll head east." Ed replaced removed the nozzle from the gas tank, placed it back on the pump, and closed the Suburban's tank. "We'll find an overpass to cross over I-95. That's the safest bet."

"It'll be dark soon," added Paul. "We should find a place to hold up for the night."

"What about right here?"

"Too close to the highway in case the deaders from up north arrive. Plus, I don't want to be here in case anyone gets the same idea we do."

Ed nodded. "Are we ready?"

Everyone piled back into the Suburban. Ed headed off on Route 123.

THEY FOUND A perfect place to spend the night less than a mile away in an old church set off from the road and surrounded by trees. There were no cars in the parking lot and no signs of deaders having been in the area. Ed stayed in the Suburban with the others in case he needed to get out of there in a hurry as Paul, Daphne, and Sparky checked out the building.

Paul knocked on the wooded door.

No sounds came from inside.

Paul knocked again, this time louder. "Is anyone in there?"

No one answered.

Sparky tried the knob. "It's locked."

"Step aside." Paul aimed his shotgun at the lock and pulled the trigger. The round removed the lock and the wood around it. Crouching, he peered inside but saw no movement.

"It's clear."

Daphne opened the door and leaned in. "If anyone's here, we don't want trouble. We're only looking for a place to stay for the night."

Again, no response.

The three entered the foyer and passed through into the nave. Paul walked down the center aisle with Sparky on the left and Daphne on the right aisles checking the pews for deaders or survivors. With the nave cleared, they swept the balcony, offices, and basement. The church was deserted.

Paul stood in front of the communion table. "Sparky, get the others. Daphne, help me set up candles around the area and light them. I don't want to turn on lights and attract people."

Fifteen minutes later, the group had set up in the nave. Daphne secured the front doors with a rope wrapped around the knobs to warn them if anyone or anything tried to get in. Becca prepared a dinner that consisted of fruit and beef jerky. After they ate, Paul gathered the group together.

"We need to set up a guard outside in case any deaders show up or anyone tries to steal the Suburban. Sparky, you stand watch until 2100. Ed will take over next and Daphne at midnight. I'll relieve her at 0300. Everyone okay with that?"

No one protested.

Once Sparky had exited, Paul unfolded a map of the eastern coast of the United States and spread it out on the alter. The adults gathered around and studied it as Toshii played with Gojira.

Paul started the conversation. "Our best bet is to head for the Delaware coast. Once we clear I-95, it's mostly farmland on the peninsula. We should have little trouble getting around."

Daphne shook her head. "The problem is going to be getting across I-95. You heard Nowack. It's a death trap."

"Our best bet is right here." Ed pointed to a portion of the map between Baltimore and Philadelphia. "It looks like the population is smaller and there'll be more country road overpasses so we can avoid having to physically cross the highway."

"That sounds good to me. Once in Delaware, we'll make

our way to the coast then head north to Maine." Paul made eye contact with the others. "Does anyone disagree?"

Akiko glanced over at Toshii and back to Paul. "Will we be safe?"

"No, but we're not safe now. Eventually those things will find us. At least if we make it to my place in New Hampshire we'll have a better chance of survival."

Akiko grimaced and nodded her approval.

"Who put you in charge?" protested Sparky.

Paul glared at him. "What's your problem?"

"You are." Sparky stiffened his back but would not dare get close to Paul. "Every decision you've made so far has almost gotten us killed."

Daphne bristled. "We're all still alive thanks to him."

Sparky shot her an icy stare. "I'm not talking to you."

Daphne started to go after Sparky but Paul stopped her.

The asshole didn't know when to quit. "Everyone is following you like sheep up to New Hampshire when it's obvious we'd be safer in Pennsylvania. I say we vote on who's in charge."

"You mean between you and Paul?" asked Ed.

"Yeah."

"Good luck with that." Ed laughed. "The difference between humans and animals is that animals would never allow the dumbest one in the pack to lead them."

For a moment, Paul thought Sparky would lunge at Ed. Finally, the teenager turned and headed for the alcove, mumbling under his breath, "Fuck all of you."

"It's settled then." Paul folded the map. "We'll leave at sunrise."

Ed took the map. "Let me study these for awhile so I have an idea what route to take."

"Be my guest."

As Ed went over the maps, everyone settled down for a much-needed sleep.

PAUL WOKE WITH a start. He sat up from the pew, his heart pounding, and scanned the area for danger as he reached for the shotgun leaning against the pew in front of him. Nothing moved in the light provided by the dozens of candles they had placed around the nave. Across the aisle, Gojira sat on the floor beneath the pew Toshii slept on. The dog raised his head at the commotion Paul made, licked his mouth, and went back to sleep. Paul calmed down. If Gojira didn't show concern, then the chances were good they were not in danger.

Paul checked his watch. It read 2:47. Almost time for shift change with Daphne. He wished he had a cup of coffee to get him going. Instead, he stood and stretched out the kinks in his back and shoulders, picked up the Mossberg, and exited through the handicap access on the side of the foyer.

Daphne sat on the step second step from the bottom of the stairs. Hearing him coming down the ramp, she reached for her Mossberg.

"It's only me."

"Good. I would have shot if it had been Sparky or a dead-er."

Paul sat beside Daphne. "You hate him that much?"

"I don't trust the bastard. If it came down to us or him, he'd abandon the group in a heartbeat."

Though Paul agreed with her, he decided to change the subject. "How was your shift?"

"Quiet."

"See anything?"

"A car drove by around one but either didn't see me or didn't care. And a family of deer wandered by fifteen minutes ago."

"They're the only ones who will benefit. With humans gone, no one will be hunting them anymore. Soon they'll be the predominant living things on the planet."

"What if the virus species jumps?"

Daphne's question jolted Paul awake quicker than a cup of espresso mixed with Red Bull. "What made you think of that?"

"It's possible."

"If that happens, we're screwed." Paul shook his head. "The thought of deader bears or coyotes is terrifying."

"I could live with that. They're already scary. Can you imagine the indignity of being attacked and devoured by a horde of deader chipmunks?"

Paul laughed aloud. "You have a morbid sense of humor. I like that."

"Aren't you glad you saved me?"

"I am."

Daphne paused. "Why did you risk your life to save me?"

"I couldn't just leave you there to die."

"I might have been a liability."

Paul refused to admit that if she had been, he would have left her behind at the strip club. "But you're not. I don't know if I'd have made it this far without you. Besides, you're useful to have around."

"Useful?"

"Bad choice of words. I should have said pleasant but, given the circumstances, that didn't seem appropriate."

"Well, in any case, I'm glad I'm with you." Daphne reached out and held his hand.

"Me, too."

"I never thanked you for saving me." Daphne stood up and faced Paul. She slid off her orange sweater. She wore a black lace bra that left little to the imagination. Dropping to her knees, Daphne unzipped Paul's pants.

"Wh… what are you doing?"

"Showing you how much I appreciate you."

Daphne smiled and lowered her head between his legs.

Chapter Eighteen

E VERYONE WOKE AN hour before dawn. Breakfast consisted of canned fruit, beef jerky, and bottled water. Once they finished eating, Ed sat on one of the pews. He pulled a small cooler between his feet, opened it, and withdrew a small bottle and a Ziploc bag filled with tiny hypodermic needles. Removing one of the latter, he pulled off the cap, inserted the needle into the bottle, and pulled back the plunger. A clear liquid filled the insides.

Toshii knelt on the pew in front of Ed, watching intently. "What are you doing?"

"I'm diabetic, son. I have to take an insulin shot every morning or I could slip into a coma."

Toshii frowned. "That sounds horrible. Having to give yourself a shot, I mean."

"You get used to it after a while." Ed slid the needle into his arm and pressed the plunger. "You can get used to anything."

"I don't know if I'll ever get used to the apocalypse."

Paul heard the conversation and wandered over. "You're diabetic?"

"Type 2." Ed placed the bottle of insulin back in the cooler between two sweaty ice packs. He disposed of the used hypodermic in a tin can. "Have been for fifteen years."

"How much insulin do you have?"

"One bottle that's open, but it won't be any good after tomorrow. It needs to be refrigerated but the ice packs have melted. I have five unused bottles. If we find a way to keep them cool, I'm set for a while. If not, then I have enough for five more days."

Paul patted his shoulder. "We'll find a way to keep them refrigerated."

"I hope so. Without the injections, you'll have to leave me behind and shoot me so I don't come back as one of those things."

"I won't let that happen."

They used the restrooms and washed up, then packed the Suburban. As the sun crested the tops of the trees, the group hit the road, with Ed driving. Shortly after leaving the church, he picked up Route 209 and headed south, switching from one back road to another as he wound his way toward Maryland.

Daphne made no public displays of affection toward Paul all morning. At first, Paul had written off last night's moment of passion as a one-night stand, which he surprisingly found himself disappointed over. He had only known her for two days but had become fond of her. He used to joke with his prepper friends on social media that a man should only get involved with a woman who could help him survive the apocalypse. Daphne certainly checked off those boxes. As the day progressed, Daphne moved closer to him until her leg pressed affectionately against his. When he glanced over to see if you, she needed more room, Daphne met his gaze with eyes filled with adoration and smiled.

Ed handed the map resting on the console to Becca. "We just entered Maryland. How far are we from I-95?"

Becca unfolded the map to their sector and studied it for a moment. "Less than two miles. Keep going straight on this road."

"Thanks." Ed slowed his speed to twenty-five miles per hour.

"Shouldn't we be speeding up?" asked Ian.

Ed shook his head and kept his attention on the road ahead. "We're too close to the interstate. I don't want to plough into a horde of those things and get trapped."

Paul surveyed the area. He couldn't see any deaders or survivors and nothing gave chase. Thank God for small miracles.

Soon after, as they crested a small hill, I-95 came into view half a mile ahead of them.

"Stop here," said Paul.

Ed braked quickly, throwing everyone forward. "Is something wrong?"

"No. I want to scout ahead and check out the underpass so we don't get ourselves in a situation we can't get out of." Paul opened the side door.

"You're not going alone?" asked Becca.

"No. Daphne and Sparky will come with me."

From the back seat, Sparky moaned. "Shit, man. Why me?"

"Because everyone does his part. Now move your ass."

As Daphne and Sparky climbed out, Paul leaned inside. "Any chance you have a pair of binoculars with you?"

"I do." Rebecca reached into her travel bag, rummaging around before removing a small pair. She rolled down her window and handed them to Paul. "They're not that powerful. I use them for bird watching."

"They're good enough. Thanks." Paul leaned to one side to see Ed. "If the shit hits the fan, get out of here and head back to that road work site a few miles back. We'll meet you there."

"If we live through it," mumbled Sparky.

Daphne punched him in the arm.

Paul closed the door and led the way to the top of the hill, their weapons in the low-ready position. Upon reaching the crest, he lay prone and raised the binoculars to his eyes. Sparky did the same on his left, using the scope on his hunting rifle to survey the area. Daphne crouched to his right, scanning the area for danger.

The interstate was a cluster fuck. Vehicles packed the

highway on both sides as far as he could see. Everyone escaping the outbreak had headed for I-95, creating gridlock. Hundreds of deaders staggered along the lanes and among the vehicles. Paul assumed everyone on this stretch had either turned into deaders or had become food. He assumed the situation was the same all along the eastern corridor. Ed had made the right call. There was no way they could cross the interstate without a tank or an armored personnel carrier.

"The underpass is blocked." Sparky lowered the hunting rifle. "But it might be passable."

Paul shifted his gaze to the underpass. The east-bound laned contained a three-car pile-up. An Amazon van had slammed into the rear end of a Prius, putting both vehicles out of commission. A Charger had rear-ended the van, the latter's back end resting on the Charger's hood. *What a waste*, thought Paul. *That would have made a kick-ass apocalypse car.* A Kawasaki motorcycle and a Taurus sat in the west-bound lanes. It looked as if the drivers stopped to help only to be killed or chased off. Only three deaders roamed around the site.

"Is it bad?" asked Daphne.

"It's not ideal, but it's nothing we can't manage." Paul handed her the binoculars. "We should be able to take out those deaders and move the other two vehicles."

"I could take them out from here," said Sparky.

Paul shook his head. "That'll create too much noise and rile up those on the interstate."

"What do you have planned?" Daphne lowered the binoculars. "Or do I not want to know?"

Paul crouch walked until they were out of sight of the underpass and led the others back to the Suburban.

"How's it look?" asked Ed.

"There's a vehicle and motorcycle blocking the left lane plus only deaders. I'll sneak down, take them down with my knife, and move the vehicles. Once the lane is clear, we should have no problems getting past."

"Are you fucking insane, man?" Sparky stepped back and raised his hands. "I ain't pulling none of that commando shit."

Paul glared at him. "No one's asking you to. I'll take care of it myself."

"We'll take care of it," added Daphne.

"It's too dangerous."

"Bullshit." Daphne moved so she faced Paul. "If you want more of last night, you're going to have to treat me like a partner and not some damsel in distress."

"You better listen to her." Becca smiled. "I can tell she's a stubborn one. I like that in a woman."

"Okay, you can come along. Ed, do you have a flashlight?"

"There's one in the glove compartment. Becca, could you get it?"

"Sure." Becca opened the compartment, fished it out, and handed it to Paul.

Paul checked the flashlight. It worked. "Once the road is clear I'll flash you three times. High-ball it before the deaders on I-95 have a chance to figure out what's going on. If you get into trouble, blare the horn and we'll come running."

Ed nodded. "Sounds good."

Ian leaned between the front seats. "Do you want me to join you?"

"I need you and Sparky here in case deaders show up. We're good." Paul turned to Daphne. "Let's go."

The two crossed over into the woods along the side of the road where they slowly and quietly made their way back to the underpass. Paul hated the idea of moving amongst the trees where any of the living dead lurking nearby could get the jump on them, but he had no choice. The three deaders around the crash site were runners. If they caught site of him and Daphne before they drew close, they would charge, forcing him and Daphne to shoot them and unravel the entire plan. After close to thirty minutes of silently maneuvering through the woods, they finally reached the overpass.

Paul crouched behind a tree. Daphne joined him. The closest deader stood fifteen feet away, swaying gently back and forth, its back to them. A second deader shambled along the road fifty feet away, facing east. The third must be farther up the road.

Paul removed the hunting knife from its sheath and whispered to Daphne. "You take out the closest one. I'll concentrate on the other two."

Daphne pulled out her knife and nodded. They made their way down the embankment and into the road.

Daphne snuck up behind the first deader. It wore a heavy leather jacket and pants. Long, unruly hair hung down its back. When within striking distance, she quietly called out, "Hey, asshole."

It turned around to face its prey. A swarm of flies and wasps covered its face. Grabbing it by the lapel of its jacket, Daphne plunged the knife into its left eye, shoving it deep until the hilt touched bone and sending the insects into flight. She twisted the blade, scrambling its brain. The deader went limp. Using the lapel, she quietly lowered the biker deader to the asphalt, removed the knife, and wiped off the blade on its t-shirt. The flies and wasps returned to their feeding.

Paul raced up behind the second deader, a young woman in a tie-dye shirt and Birkenstocks, its right arm stripped of flesh and muscle. He grabbed it by its long blonde hair. The deader started to snarl, its cry cut off when Paul drove the hunting knife between the base of its skull and its spine and twisted. The deader spasmed for a moment then collapsed. Still clasping its hair, he controlled its fall, letting it drop quietly onto the road.

The third deader, a chubby male in an Amazon delivery uniform, spun around at the noise. It lunged at Paul. He removed the knife and took a fighting stance to face the new threat. Paul surged forward at the last second, aiming for its left eye. His aim was off by inches and the knife entered its mouth, slicing across its tongue and lodging in the back of its throat.

Maggots dropped from between its lips. Congealed blood poured from the wounds, dripping out of the sides of its mouth and down its windpipe, turning the snarl into a hideous gurgle. It bit down on the blade, shattering its teeth. Paul grabbed it by the shirt, trying to hold it back, but its weight and momentum threatened to knock him off balance.

Daphne ran up and shoved her knife into its left ear, not stopping until the hilt slammed into its lobe. The Amazon deader's murky eyes rolled into its head and the thing went limp. Paul lowered it to the ground and dragged it over to the three cars, clearing the way, then stepped back to get away from the agitated insects.

They waited and listened. None of the deaders on the interstate had heard them.

Paul ran over to the female deader and dragged its body beside the Amazon deader. He handed Daphne the flashlight.

"You move the motorcycle and I'll take care of the Taurus. Once the road is clear, signal Ed."

As Daphne pushed the Kawasaki behind the pile-up, Paul jumped into the driver's seat of the Taurus. The keys were still in the ignition. He started the Taurus, pulled forward, swung it behind the wreck, and shut off the engine. By the time he joined Daphne, she had already signaled Ed that the way was clear. The Suburban made its way toward them.

Snarling came from above. The sound of something heavy falling onto metal echoed from behind them.

Chapter Nineteen

P AUL SPUN AROUND. Dozens of deaders leaned over the
guardrail of the southern-bound lanes of the interstate,
clutching at them with dead hands.

A deader in a yellow road worker's vest had toppled over
the guardrail and landed on top of the Amazon van. It
struggled to get up, slipped, and fell onto the asphalt beside
them. As it climbed to its feet, Paul swung the Vepr off his
shoulder and fired. The road worker's head exploded, plaster-
ing the Amazon logo in blood, skull fragments, and gore.

Another deader, this one a middle-aged man in a Boston
Red Sox sweatshirt, fell over the guardrail and landed head-
first onto the road, snapping its neck. The body remained
motionless but its head stared at them, clasping its teeth.

Three more fell from the interstate. One bounced off the
roof of the Amazon van and slammed into the concrete wall in
the eastbound lane. A teenage deader with no shirt and half its
chest eaten away landed in the center of the westbound lane.
Its right leg snapped on impact. It tried to rise but fell over to
one side. A pregnant female deader landed on its stomach to
the latter's right and staggered to its feet. The fall had ruptured
its amniotic sack. Fluid covered its abdomen and legs. The
dead fetus dropped from the gaping wound between the
deaders feet, still attached to the umbilical cord.

Paul blasted away the female deader's head and shifted aim
to the crippled deader, splattering its head across the road. He
raced forward and pulled each body to the side so the Subur-

ban could get through.

Daphne turned around. Ed was still a thousand feet away and approaching fast.

Another of the living dead dropped behind her. She spun around. A deader in a dress shirt and tie climbed to its feet. The bones in its right arm had splintered, the humerus having punctured the skin. It reached out its left hand and lunged. Daphne raised her Mossberg and fired, the round tearing open its chest. She raised the shotgun and fired again, only then realizing she was out of ammo. Another deader tumbled off the interstate, landing on the first. Daphne used the opportunity to switch out the empty magazine with a full one, then took down the two deaders as they tried to stand.

More deaders toppled over the guardrail, frantic to get at the food below. Some were immobilized by the fall. The others rose and went after Paul and Daphne, who took down as many as they could, but the odds were against them. The deaders would overrun them in seconds.

A deader in a Maryland State Police uniform raced at Daphne from the right. The Suburban slammed into it, propelling it fifty feet down the road. Ian opened the back door.

"Get in."

Daphne pumped a round into a teenage deader rushing toward them then jumped into the middle seat. Paul took down three more approaching rapidly then followed. He was halfway in when a female deader in a running suit landed on his back, pushing him to the floor. Paul shoved his head back, shattering its nose and knocking out two teeth, stunning it for a moment. A stinging erupted on the back of his scalp. He twisted to the side and slammed his elbow into the side of its head, loosening its grip. Rolling over, Paul kicked at the deader, pushing it halfway out of the opening. It grabbed onto the door and interior jamb, still snarling and biting.

A deader wearing a baseball cap and blue trucker's vest ran

along the right front of the Suburban, hoping to join in the feeding frenzy. Becca waited until it reached her then pushed open the front door. The blow knocked it backward onto the pavement.

Other deaders were closing in on the Suburban. Daphne and Ian attempted to line up shots on the runner deader but risked shooting Paul if they fired. From the backseat, Sparky withdrew his Glock, leaned forward, and placed the barrel against the side of its head. He fired a single round, shattering its skull. Paul placed both legs against its chest and shoved, throwing the runner deader against the Amazon van. He crawled into the Suburban and closed the door before a deader, its face eaten away, slammed into the side, its bloody face smearing the window.

"Go!"

Ed accelerated. The Suburban shot forward, bouncing over bodies and pulling away from the horde, which gave chase. He was halfway through the underpass when deaders tumbled over the guardrail in the northbound lanes of the interstate. He rammed one that stood up directly in front of the vehicle, throwing it to one side where it slammed into the Taurus.

As he exited the underpass, three more deaders toppled off I-95. One crashed onto the asphalt to the left, its head rupturing. The second smashed into the windshield, fracturing the glass in a spider web pattern, before rolling off to the side. The third landed on the hood. It grabbed on with one hand and punched the windshield with the other, weakening the already damaged glass.

Ed hit the brakes. The deader lost its grip and slid down the hood, disappearing in front of the Suburban. As it stood, Ed accelerated, ramming it. As it went under the vehicle, it grabbed onto the bumper and was dragged along. The asphalt ripped off the back of its clothes and grated its skin. It refused to let go, the rough ride bouncing its body against the engine. The check engine light came on and the temperature gauge began to inch its way toward the red zone. A rattling came from under the hood. After three hundred feet, the deader could not hold on any longer and released its grip. The Suburban bounced over the body, jarring everyone inside.

Ed continued down the road, praying he could put significant distance between themselves and the rampaging horde behind them before the engine gave out.

Paul shifted in his seat toward Sparky. "Thanks. You saved my life back there."

Rather than just accept the gratitude, Sparky replied, "If those things had gotten in here, we'd all be dead."

"You're welcome would have been sufficient."

Daphne leaned closer and touched the back of Paul's head.

"What are you doing?" asked Paul.

"Checking your scalp. I want to make sure you weren't bit when you head butted that thing."

Everyone in back leaned away from Paul. Sparky tightened his grip on the revolver.

After several anxious seconds, Daphne stopped rummaging through his hair and hugged him from behind. "You're fine. Just a wasp bite."

"Thank God."

She smiled at him. "Sometimes it's good to be hardheaded."

Paul squeezed her hand. He glanced out the back. The deaders that had been chasing them were no where in sight. Paul turned to face forward.

"Where are we now?"

Becca consulted the map. "According to this, we're about ten miles from the coast."

Chapter Twenty

E D OPTED NOT to drive to the eastern coast because of all the populated areas between them and the shore. Instead, he followed Route 123 south through the countryside with the intention of finding a boatyard somewhere along the southern shore. At the junction north of the town of Kennedyville, Ed slowed to a stop.

"Anything wrong?" asked Paul.

Ed pointed ahead of him. "Looks like we can't go any further."

A tractor trailer sat across the road, the front and back ends resting on both shoulders. A pair of wooden barriers stood in front of the truck, one in each lane. Someone had hung a slab of plywood off the trailer and painted on it the words:

DANGER!!!
HEAVY DEADER ACTIVTY IN CHARLESTOWN AND
KINGSTOWN
SEEK ALTERNATE ROUTES

"Shit," said Daphne.

"We can't go that way." Ed sighed, the frustration evident in his tone. "We're being boxed in out here."

"I'm on it." Becca spread the map on the dashboard and studied it, then pointed to the road on the right. "Take 298. That'll take us closer to the shore. It comes out at Rock Hall Harbor. Hopefully, we'll find a boat there."

"Good," agreed Paul. "We need to get off the roads. We're

too vulnerable out here.

"Rock Hall Harbor it is." Ed turned onto the back road.

Twenty miles later, the rattling of the engine became more pronounced and the Suburban began bucking. Steam rose from under the hood.

"Damn it," mumbled Ed.

Paul leaned forward. "What's wrong?"

"Our run in with the deaders at the underpass fucked up the engine. This is far as we go."

"Can you fix it?"

"Let's look."

Paul and Ed climbed out to check on the engine. The others joined them to stretch their legs or, in Gojira's case, to pee on a road sign.

Ed popped the lock and lifted the hood. An ungodly stench wafted from the engine that smelled like charred flesh. Ed waved his hand to clear away the steam and bent over to per inside, quickly withdrawing his head.

"For God fucking sake."

Curiosity got the better of Paul. He approached the right fender and looked. The deader at the underpass that had lodged under the front of the Suburban had ruptured its abdomen. Somehow its intestines had become caught in the fan blades and unwound, wrapping around the shaft and seizing it up. The water hose leading to the radiator had been torn loose. Without the fan and a supply of water, the engine had overheated.

Daphne and Toshii came over and peeked in. Daphne grimaced. Toshii broke out into a grin and responded, "Awesome!"

Paul rubbed Toshii's head and focused on Ed. "Can it be repaired?"

Ed studied the mess. "I could clear the fan of intestines. It should work okay unless the shaft is bent. The problem is the torn hose." He reached in, grabbed the loose end, and pulled it toward the radiator. "There's not much left to re-attach. It won't hold for long, especially if we run into any more of those things."

"We're not far from the pier, right?" asked Daphne.

"Two miles," replied Ed. "Three at most."

"That settles it." Paul closed the hood. "We walk the rest of the way. Let's grab our gear."

Popping open the rear hatch, Paul removed the two backpacks, placing one by his feet and giving the second to Sparky. Ed opened the cooler. The ice packs had melted, but the water remained cool. Ed slipped the unopened bottles of insulin into his jacket pocket then removed a needle from the Ziploc bag of hypodermics before placing the bag in the same pocket. He used the needle to inject himself with a shot from the used insulin bottle before the contents went bad.

Paul turned to the others. "Everyone, show me what you have left for ammo."

Those carrying firearms emptied their pockets and placed their ammunition on the Suburban's back deck. They had thirty-seven rounds for the Vepr and Mossberg, forty-one for the Glocks, eighteen for the .38, nine for the Magnum, and sixteen for the hunting rifle. Paul divided the shotgun bullets evenly between himself and Daphne and the Glock rounds between him and Sparky.

"We're running low, so use it sparingly. We don't know when we'll have a chance to stock up again. Which way to the harbor?"

Becca pointed south. "That way."

"Let's go."

THE MAIN ROAD into Rock Hall Harbor went through the center of town, with deaders roaming the streets. Vehicles sat abandoned along the sides of the road, their doors open, blood smearing the interior. The remains of those who failed to make it into town lay on the street. Paul led them south around the outskirts of town, looking for an easy approach to the harbor. After several hours of walking and avoiding the living dead, they finally crested a hill to the south of Rock Hall Harbor overlooking the town.

Ed summed up the disappointment they all felt when he muttered, "Dammit."

Deaders inundated the northern half of Rock Hall Harbor. Cars packed the parking lots, now surrounded by the living dead. Everyone in the area had the same idea—grab a boat and escape the outbreak by sea. Most didn't make it. Over a hundred corpses floated around the marina, turning the water crimson. Close to two dozen boats remained tied to the pier, most small pleasure craft used for cruising Chesapeake Bay and too small to carry all of them, let alone be of much use out on the ocean. A wall of deaders surrounded the three or four left behind that could meet their needs, far too many to fight their way through. A ferry had come in to rescue survivors, but to no avail. It floated in the center of the harbor, its decks awash with the living dead.

The southern piers lay across the harbor but would be of little use. Being smaller, all the boats docked their had made their escape. A single canoe was moored to one piling, a devoured body laying inside. Three dozen of the living dead hovered around the canoe or wandered the piers.

"We're fucked," said Sparky.

"The other side of the bay isn't that far away," suggested Akiko. "Couldn't we use the canoe to get across?"

Paul shook his head. "We'd have to make several trips to ferry everyone across. Plus, we'd have to expend most of our ammo clearing the way, which would attract the deaders from the north. Anyone left behind would be overrun before the canoe could get back to them."

Daphne moved beside Paul and clasped his hand. "What

now?"

He did not have an answer.

A breakwater extended from the bottom of the hill and into the harbor.

"Sparky and I will go to the end of that and see if we can see anything from there that might be of use." Paul met Daphne's gaze, his eyes warning her not to argue. "You stay here and protect the others. We'll be back in a few minutes."

Daphne squeezed his hand. "Be careful."

"We will. Don't worry."

The two men proceeded down the hill.

Daphne watched them go. "I don't trust Sparky. If there's trouble, he'll ditch Paul and save his own life."

"I agree with you there," said Ed as he moved up alongside her. "That boy's dick is so small he could fuck a Cheerio."

NO DEADERS LINGERED around the breakwater or the area. Paul and Sparky moved slowly so if any of the living dead noticed them, they would think the moving bodies were one of them. As they neared the end, Sparky stopped and stared out over the bay.

"You've got to be fucking kidding."

Paul agreed with the sentiment.

Ten miles away, the twin spans of the Chesapeake Bay Bridge scanned the water, connecting the eastern and western shores, each span just over four and a half miles long and with a two-hundred-feet clearance above the bay. Even from this distance, it was clear deaders packed the southern span.

Chapter Twenty-One

THREE HOURS LATER, the group gathered around the broken-down Suburban planning their next course of action while they ate dinner. Toshii played with Gojira.

"Okay," protested Sparky. "You screwed the pooch on this one."

"Fuck you," snapped Daphne, coming to Paul's defense.

Sparky ignored her. "What other great ideas do you have?"

Paul glared at him. "I don't hear you coming up with anything better."

"Yeah? Well, how about we backtrack to Pennsylvania where there were fewer deaders and head west from there?"

Ed shook his head. "We'd have to cross I-95 again."

"We almost didn't make it last time." Akiko had a tone of fear to her voice.

"Even if we decide on that option, we don't have a car," Ed reminded everyone.

"There were several abandoned ones outside Rock Hall Harbor."

"As well as a pack of deaders," added Akiko.

Daphne shook her head. "The asshole is right about one thing."

Sparky flipped her his middle finger, which Daphne paid no attention to. "No matter what we do, we need a car to get out of here."

"We need two," corrected Paul. "We have too much gear and people to fit into one SUV. What are our options besides going back to Pennsylvania?"

Paul thought a moment. "What if we go back to mainland and head south before we reach the interstate?"

Becca studied the map. "No good. Baltimore is just south of here. The coast roads run through the city. And the only way to get through the center of town is an underground tunnel."

Sparky shook his head. "Fuck that. We'd never make it."

"Agreed." Paul sighed. "Other options?"

Becca ran her fingers north. "There are several bridges on the main roads west of Baltimore."

"Those are probably packed with deaders as well."

"And to do that, we'd still need to cross I-95," added Ed.

Daphne jumped in. "That limits us to heading east to the coast."

Becca sighed. "We'd have to cross at least one main highway. Even if we succeeded in doing that, the Maryland coast is heavily populated. We would run into hundreds of deaders."

"What about crossing over the bay bridges?" asked Daphne, desperate for a solution.

Sparky shook his head. "The span is packed with deaders. We'd never make it."

"Maybe we could use that canoe we saw in Rock Hall Harbor?" suggested Akiko.

"Too many deaders around it. We'd get killed trying."

Akiko would not give up. "Suppose someone swam to it and brought it to the breakwater? There were no deaders there."

The group contemplated the idea but Paul shut it down. "I don't like the idea of separating the group while we ferry people across. It's too dangerous if we're attacked."

"I'm willing to take the risk," said Sparky.

"I'm not." Paul paused, not sure if he should mention this. "While Sparky and I were examining the bridges, I noticed the eastern one, the suspension bridge, was closed for road work. It had several large construction vehicles on it but no traffic."

"And no traffic means no deaders," added Daphne.

"Or, at worst, enough that we can easily handle."

Becca folded her hands in prayer. "God knew we were due for a break. Maybe this is it."

Ian agreed. "If Paul's right, and the suspension bridge is closed for repairs, we shouldn't have too much trouble getting across."

"What if he's wrong?" Sparky snorted. "What if it's as packed as everything else?"

Paul shrugged. "Then we'll continue to the coast of Maryland and keep searching until we find a boat."

Sparky seemed dumfounded. "We're doing this?"

"Let's take a vote. Who's for heading back to central Pennsylvania?"

Sparky raised his hand.

"Who's for heading for the coast?"

Akiko and Becca raised theirs.

"And crossing the bridge?"

Paul raised his along with Daphne, Ed, and Toshii.

Sparky threw his arms in the air. "This is nuts."

"You're welcome to set out on your own." Daphne had a tone of hopefulness mixed with contempt in her voice.

The teenager sighed. "If I'm gonna die, at least I'll have the satisfaction of proofing Paul is an ass."

Becca had gone back to examining the map. "It's a good fifty mile walk to the bridge. And that includes the stretch of Route 50 leading to the ramps. That's a long walk."

Daphne nudged Paul. "I think we can fix that."

PAUL AND DAPHNE waited until sundown before heading back to Rock Hall Harbor. A dozen vehicles were abandoned on the outskirts of town with minimal deader activity, so they reasoned it would be their best chance of commandeering a

SCOTT M. BAKER

vehicle. If their luck held.

The first car they came across was a Subaru Forester with a
flat tire. Daphne checked inside.

"The keys are still in the ignition."

"Keep it as a back-up in case we find nothing better. We'll
attract to much attention if we change out the tire. We'll use it
as a last resort."

Three hundred yards further ahead were a Chevy Malibu
and a Toyota Tacoma. The first was too small to carry them
all. The Toyota would be perfect except that two deaders
shambled around it, a female deader in a cheerleader's uniform
by the rear bed and another by the driver's door.

"You up to this?" asked Paul.

"There's only two of them." Daphne smiled. "You're going
soft on me."

"You only need one to get bitten. Let's go."

They approached from behind the Malibu, using the car as
a shield. Crouching by the right rear fender, Paul peered
around the vehicle. Neither deader had noticed them. Paul
withdrew his hunting knife then leaned close to whisper.

"You take the one in back. I'll get the one by the door."

Daphne kissed him. "Be careful."

The two moved around the right side of the Malibu and
quietly made their way to the Toyota. Paul stayed behind
Daphne in case she ran into trouble and needed help. She
didn't.

Daphne circled around behind the cheerleader deader,
sneaking up without making a sound. Before it knew what had
happened, she had wrapped her fingers around its long, gore-
filled hair, pushed its head forward, and plunged the blade
between its spine and skull. The deader stiffened then went
limp. Daphne lowered it onto the asphalt.

Paul rushed past her. Only then did he notice that his
deader had been a member of a police team and still wore its
riot control helmet with the faceplate down. It made a slow,

shambling turn. On seeing Paul, it raced forward. The noise would attract the other deaders if he didn't shut it up. Paul grabbed the base of the helmet and shoved his hunting knife into its throat, punching through to the larynx. The snarl became a gurgle. It snapped its teeth, unable to reach him through the faceplate. Paul pulled out the knife, turned the blade up, and drove it through the deader's lower jaw. It punctured the palate and imbedded in the frontal lobe. The deader's eyes bulged. Paul turned his hand, twisting the blade around inside its skull. A second later, the deader went limp. Paul shoved the body against the side of the Tacoma and slid it quietly to the ground, then paused to listen.

A murmur came from the deaders farther down the road. One turned in the direction of the Tacoma but, hearing no sounds or seeing no movement, resumed its shambling toward Rock Hall Harbor.

A hand clasped his shoulder. Paul jumped until he realized Daphne had joined him.

"You scared the shit out of me."

Daphne crinkled her nose and grinned. "Not a pleasant image."

Paul leaned into the cab. Luckily, the keys were in the ignition. He climbed in, turned the key to the auxiliary setting, and shifted into reverse. Jumping out, he ushered Daphne inside.

"You steer while I push."

"Why don't we just start it and get the hell out of here?"

"The noise will attract every deader in town. I want to put some distance between us first."

Ten minutes later, Paul climbed into the passenger seat. Daphne started the engine, made a three-point turn, and headed back to the Suburban. The others climbed in, Ed, Becca, and Akiko in the backseat with Sparky and Toshii in the bed along with Gojira and their backpacks. Daphne retraced their path back to the roadblock and picked up Route 213 heading to the Bay Bridges.

Chapter Twenty-Two

T HE ONLY WAY to get to the approaches to the bridge was to cross Route 301, the main highway, and drive through the towns heading south. Daphne crossed Route 301 at an overpass in Queenstown. She slowed to study the highway. The traffic attempting to reach the twin bridges was backed up beyond Queenstown. Thousands of deaders shambled between the abandoned vehicles. The northbound lane was relatively empty, which would make their approach to the bay easier. Several dozen deaders noticed them and gave chase, unable to reach the Tacoma.

Daphne turned onto Route 18, sped past Queenstown, and headed for the bridges.

Grasonville contained a fair number of deaders along the main route. Thankfully, the roads were clear of traffic. Switching off the headlights, Daphne raced through the town, using the streetlamps to navigate. Half a dozen of the living dead chased them but, after a few miles, she had left them far behind.

Route 18 veered right and paralleled the highway for a quarter of a mile. Thousands of deaders milled through the gridlock on the southbound side of Route 301. The only lights came from the headlights of those vehicles whose batteries had not yet died and the streetlamps on the approaches. Daphne decelerated and cruised along as quietly as possible. Some deaders picked up the sounds of the Tacoma's engine, their heads jerking from side to side, but could not locate it. Up ahead, the road turned left. No living dead were around.

Daphne stopped the Tacoma. An exit ramp sat in front of them and, a few hundred feet beyond that, the approaches to the suspension bridge across Chesapeake Bay. Jersey barriers divided the northbound from the southbound lanes, isolating the deaders to the opposite side. The area where the northern traffic merged back into its proper lanes occurred half a mile to their right, which meant no deaders were around. Daphne shut off the engine.

"Everyone out and remain quiet."

A loud clap of thunder greeted them as exited the Tacoma. On the other side of the bay, a storm slowly approached, the front hovering over Annapolis.

"Shit," complained Sparky. "Figures it's going to rain."

"Good," sighed Paul, fed up with Sparky's bullshit. "The noise will provide additional cover."

Becca stared at the bridge, shivering.

"Are you cold?" asked Ed. "Do you want my jacket?"

"I'm scared of heights."

Ed placed an arm around Becca's shoulder and hugged her. "We'll stay in the center. It's night. You won't even notice."

Paul helped Toshii and Gojira out of the bed then handed out the backpacks. "Don't talk and stay as far to the left as possible. If we run into any deaders, try to take them down quietly. We don't want to rile up the others. Is everyone ready?"

The group nodded.

"Let's go."

They made their way up the ramp and moved toward the suspension bridge. Except for the occasional rumble of thunder and the moaning it created among the living dead on the opposite side, everything remained quiet. Then a tapping on glass shattered the stillness. Paul glanced to his right. A black limousine rested against the jersey barrier heading north. In the back, a blonde woman banged on the rear window and yelled, "Help me."

The noise attracted the attention of the nearby deaders which rushed toward the limousine.

Sparky raised his hunting rifle but didn't fire. "Dumb bitch will get us all killed."

"What are we going to do about her?" asked Daphne.

"I think I can save her," said Paul. "The rest of you go on without me. I'll catch up."

"I'm not leaving you alone."

Paul clasped her hand. "I need you to lead the others across the bridge. I can't leave her here."

Daphne kissed him on the cheek. "Please don't do anything foolish."

As the others ducked low and ran down the span, Paul waved until he caught the blonde's attention. He held up a finger and mouthed the word, "I'll be back in a minute."

She banged and screamed even louder as Paul ran away, unintentionally attracting attention to the limousine. He returned to the Tacoma, pulled two of the plastic gas containers from the bed, then fished around in the glove compartment for a lighter. Nothing. He opened the plastic toolbox mounted on the front wall of the bed, discovering three road flares nestled inside. Shoving the flares in his back pocket, Paul headed back to the limousine with the gas containers.

Close to a hundred deaders packed around the limo. Paul unscrewed the lids then tossed the gasoline from one container on the trunk and the deaders swarming around its rear. He used the second to do the same thing with the hood. A torrential rain started to fall, the droplets pounding on the roofs of the other vehicles, providing a brief distraction. Paul prayed this would work.

Igniting a flare, he tossed it onto the trunk. The flame ignited the gasoline, creating a small inferno that engulfed the rear of the limousine and over twenty of the living dead. Hundreds of insects ignited in the pyre, their death throes creating sparkling corpses that dropped on the roof of the limousine. One deader in a suit stood blocking the rear door, its jacket shredded and blood staining its white shirt crimson. Paul took it down with a single shot to the head.

He waved to the blonde. "Hurry."

To her credit, she didn't panic. The blonde opened the door but it moved only two feet before the edge slammed into the jersey barrier.

"I can't get out."

"Close the door and duck."

Paul blasted out the rear window with a single round from the Vepr. "Give me your hands."

The blonde crawled halfway out the window and clasped Paul by the wrists. He pulled her out of the limousine, across the cement barrier, and onto the asphalt. Shards of glass fell off her knee-length red dress.

"Thanks for saving me. I'm Lisa."

"No time for that now. We've gotta get moving."

Lisa kicked off her high heels and fell in behind Paul.

The gasoline tank of the limo exploded a minute later, wrecking the vehicles around it and killing or incapacitating close to a hundred of the living dead. However, the commotion had attracted thousands more. They rushed to the jersey barriers, clutching at Paul and Lisa. Some dropped over the side, stumbled to their feet, and gave chase. Within minutes, three hundred deaders rushed along the suspension bridge toward them.

Damn it, thought Paul. *I Charlie Foxtrotted this one.*

Halfway across the bridge, where the first and second set of main cables merged, Paul and Lisa came upon the rest of the group who had stopped.

"Keep running," he yelled. "They're behind us."

"We can't," yelled Daphne.

Sparky added, "The fucking bridge is gone."

Paul saw what the asshole referred to and his heart sank. A two hundred-foot-section running the width of the bridge had been dug up, leaving an uncrossable gap. He spun around. A horde of deaders raced toward them and were a quarter of a mile away.

They were trapped.

Chapter Twenty-Three

"**W**E'RE DEAD BECAUSE you had to save the bitch," snapped Sparky.

Paul said nothing because he knew Sparky was right. By saving Lisa, he had condemned them all to death.

Toshii walked up with Gojira. "Mr. Madison, have you ever played *Assassin's Creed?*"

Akiko hugged her son. "Not now."

Paul motioned that it was okay to let Toshii speak. "I don't play video games."

"There's a level where the main character has to cross a bridge guarded by soldiers. It's almost impossible to fight your way through them. I beat the level by silently crossing the bridge on the supports above the span." Toshii pointed to the main cable. "If we can't cross the bridge, why don't we go over it?"

Sparky huffed. "Are you really going to take—?"

Paul cut him off. As insane as it sounded, it was their only chance. "Everyone, start climbing. Daphne, you go first and take Akiko and Toshii."

"What about Gojira?" cried Toshii.

"He won't make it and we can't carry him. He's too big."

"But—"

"Toshii, your mother needs you. Please."

Toshii hugged the dog, who barked once, then joined his mother and Daphne.

Daphne had already climbed onto the guard rail, refusing

to look down at the bay two hundred feet below. The rain made the metal casing around the suspension cables slippery. Nor did the winds from the approaching storm help. Daphne gripped the small cables used as handrails until her knuckles turned white and ascended. She never completely released her hold, clutching desperately to a cable with one hand as the other slid along its counterpart. Her feet kept wanting to slide out from under her. There were no flat surfaces or padding to give her a better foothold, and the shoes she wore only made the climb more difficult. In the darkness of the night, she could not even see the top of the tower, only the flashing red aviation warning lights cutting through the rain. Daphne regretted doing this but had already made the commitment.

She turned around to check on the others. Akiko and Toshii had not followed.

"Hurry up," Daphne urged. "It's the only way."

Toshii ran up ten feet then called to Akiko. "Come on, Mom. It's not that bad."

Akiko joined them, moving slow and uncertainly.

Gojira moved over beside Paul but kept staring at Toshii.

The horde was only an eighth of a mile away.

"Ed, you're next. Take Becca and Lisa."

"I can't." Becca turned to Ed. "I'm terrified of heights."

Lisa took Becca by the arm and maneuvered her toward the suspension cable. "Come on. You don't want to die here. Trust me."

As Lisa slid off her pantyhose, Ed ushered Becca onto the guardrail.

"Just put one foot in front of the other and make sure you hold on tight to the side cables."

"I... can't. Leave me."

"No."

"I don't want you to die."

"Then you better start climbing because I'm staying with you no matter what." Ed spoke the words in a firm but comforting voice.

"Hurry up before we get swarmed." Sparky emphasized his point by shooting one of the approaching deaders.

Becca placed her left foot on the suspension cable and clutched the hand cables for dear life. She placed her right foot on the suspension cable and began the slow climb.

Lisa jumped on when there was space and turned around. "It's clear."

The deaders were three hundred feet away.

"You go first," said Paul.

Sparky ran off, jumped onto the guardrail, and rushed up as far as Lisa.

The deaders were one hundred feet away. This would be close.

Paul raced over, vaulted onto the guardrail, and climbed. Out of the corner of his eye, he saw Gojira run to the eastern most guardrail and past the swarm, which ignored him. He hoped the dog would be okay.

Paul had made it only a yard when a deader in a waitress uniform jumped up on the guardrail and faced him. A second deader in a postal delivery uniform followed, knocking them both off the bridge. They snarled on the way down until their bodies smashed into the bay below.

A deader in a white shirt and black tie reached the side of the suspension cable and jumped, catching Paul by the left leg and knocking him off balance. He fell onto the casing and slid down the side, his grip on the hand cable the only thing preventing him from falling back onto the bridge. The deader hung on tight, wrapping its other hands around Paul's ankle. Dozens more swarmed around it, hoping to share in the feast. Paul thrashed his left leg around, praying the deader would not bite him, and kicked out with his right. His foot caught the white-shirted deader in the face. He repeated the attack but it refused to let go. Holding on tight with his left hand, Paul fumbled for the Magnum with his right.

"Sparky!"

A teenage deader with long, scraggly hair covered in gore climbed onto the base of the suspension cable and paused, snarling at him. It lunged. Paul withdrew the Magnum and fired blindly. The bullet slammed into its chest with enough force to knock it off balance. The body toppled over and slid lengthwise down the suspension cable, becoming caught in the vertical supports at the bottom and blocking the others from coming after him. An increasing number of deaders massed around it, trying to get up on the suspension cable. The mound grew to ten feet in height before the top layer of living dead collapsed off the side of the bridge.

Paul shifted his attention to those gathered around his legs. He aimed and fired a single round at the white-shirted deader that struck hit it in the temple, blasting off the opposite side of its head. With the grip released, Paul kicked away the other grasping for him and spider-walked up the cable until he was out of danger. He then scrambled to his feet and continued after the others.

"Hey, asshole."

Sparky glanced over his shoulder.

"Why didn't you come and help me?"

"I didn't know you were in trouble."

"You didn't here me call for help or the gunshots?"

"No."

Fucking bullshit, Paul thought.

I'LL NEVER LISTEN to anyone under eighteen again.

Daphne wanted to slap Toshii for even suggesting this, though they'd all be dead by now if he hadn't. She knew taking this route would not be easy but never expected it to be this terrifying. The faster she moved, the more her feet wanted to slide off. She slowed down to make the ascent safer, but that only prolonged the ordeal. Even worse, the higher they climbed the steeper the slope became. Earlier, she had made the mistake of looking down. Though she could not see the surface, she made out the whitecaps blown up by the storm rippling across the water. They had to be at least four hundred feet above the bay. The thought paralyzed her with fear. Daphne closed her eyes and forced herself to think about something else. Her mind focused on the bridge in Pittsburgh and how her failure to act had almost cost her life then. She refused to let that happen again. Paul had snapped her out of her inactivity back then. It was time to pay it forward.

She paused and glanced over her shoulder. Toshii seemed to be taking this in stride, a typical teenager enjoying the adventure. Akiko, on the other hand, crawled along at a snail's pace. Daphne waited until the two caught up before proceeding.

They had climbed another one hundred feet when Akiko cried out. She had tripped over a cable clamp, causing her to lose balance. She wrapped both arms around the hand cable and held it tight against her chest, too frozen with fear to go on.

"Are you okay, Mom?"

"I can't do this anymore. Go ahead with Daphne."

"I'm not leaving you."

Daphne cautiously turned around. "Akiko, look at me."

The woman slowly raised her head, her eyes wide with terror, her lower jaw quivering.

"If Toshii and I can do this, so can you."

"I'm scared."

"We all are. You can do this."

"I can't." Akiko clutched the cable tighter. "Please take care of Toshii for me."

"My cat ran away from me I'm such a bad parent. Besides, Toshii needs his mother."

Akiko met Toshii's gaze. He nodded in agreement.

"Come on, Akiko. We're halfway there," Daphne lied, knowing they had barely made it a third of the way to the top.

SCOTT M. BAKER

Akiko took three long breaths then carefully stood, testing her footing. She finally said, "Let's go."

The three continued their way to the top.

"YOU'RE DOING GREAT," encouraged Ed.

"How high up do you think we are?"

"Who cares? Just focus on me."

"I'm right behind you for support," added Lisa.

The rain came down heavier, pounding against the bridge supports and stinging their faces. The three plodded along.

PAUL AND SPARKY caught up with Ed and the women, slowly down to match their pace. They had climbed another fifty feet when Sparky mumbled, "Fuck this shit."

Sparky surged ahead.

"What the fuck are you doing?" asked Paul.

"They're too slow."

"Stop being an asshole."

Sparky ignored him. He tapped Lisa on the shoulder.

"Let me by."

Lisa removed her right hand from the guardrail. Sparky stepped past her.

"Dickhead," she mumbled.

"Knock it off," yelled Paul.

Sparky tapped Becca on the shoulder. "Excuse me."

"Piss off."

Sparky grabbed Becca's right wrist and forcefully removed her hand from the cable, then shoved past. Becca's right foot slipped. Her body twisted left and she slid off the main cable. She had enough common sense not to release her left hand from the cable. Becca dangled precariously off the bridge, kicking and screaming.

"Help me!"

The deaders on the northern approaches churned themselves into a frenzy.

Lisa rushed forward, stretched her left arm over the cable, and grabbed Becca's wrist in both hands. Ed ran back and sat on the suspension cable, wrapping both legs around a vertical support cable. Holding on with his right hand, he reached out with his left but could not get hold of her flailing arm.

"Hold still so I can take your hand."

Becca reached her right arm behind her head, still thrashing it about. Ed finally caught it in his left hand and reached around with his right, clasping his fingers in hers to get a better grip. Becca still kicked her legs and screamed.

"Hold still or we'll drop you," yelled Lisa.

It did no good. Panic had taken over Becca's senses. Neither Lisa or Ed had the strength or the footing to pull up Becca.

Sparky continued up the suspension cable.

"Paul," shouted Ed. "We need help."

Paul moved over beside Lisa. He planted his feet firmly on the anchor bolt, reached both arms over the hand cable, and clutched Becca's left hand in his own.

"I got her."

Lisa let go. Paul immediately clutched Becca's wrist in his right hand. Lisa carefully stood and moved away.

"Becca," he yelled. "Stop moving. We can't hold you."

Ed leaned over the cables and reached out but could get hold of Becca's arm.

"Can you pull her up a little?"

Paul strained, his arm muscles growing weak, but managed to lift Becca enough that Ed was able to clasp her around the wrist.

"I got her."

Becca, thinking she was falling, thrashed around violently, screaming at the top of her lungs. Both men pulled her in. They had her up to the cable when Becca's leg kicked out against the main cable, propelling her body forward and breaking Paul's grip. Only Ed held her now. The added weight and whipping around caught him off guard. Her weight dragged him over the cable.

"I'll get her," Paul called out.

He dropped prone on the main cable and reached out for Becca but she was to overcome with fear to help. She thrashed about, yanking Ed off the suspension the cable. He let go of Becca and wrapped his arms around the vertical support, preventing him from falling. Becca cried out as she plummeted toward the bay. Her body slammed into one of the girders along the span, bursting like a water balloon and covering the metal with blood before tumbling into the water hundreds of feet below.

Ed swung himself back on the suspension cable and found his footing.

"That son of a bitch."

Ed set off after Sparky but Paul grabbed his arm. "Enough."

"That asshole killed her." Tears formed in Ed's eyes, though they were hard to see because of the rain.

"We'll discuss this later. Right now, we need to get off this bridge."

Paul made his way to the front of the line and continued his ascent. Ed and Lisa fell in behind him.

DAPHNE REACHED THE top of the tower. Still holding the ends of the cables, she placed her foot on the surface and assessed it, then glanced over her shoulder.

"Be careful. It's slippery up here. But we should be okay."

Turning around, she helped Toshii onto the top of the tower, then both assisted Akiko. Once off the main cable, she fell onto the metal and sobbed.

Toshii knelt and hugged her. "I told you we'd make it."

Akiko embraced him tight. "We still have to get down the

other side."

That was something Daphne did not want to think about.

The storm had reached its peak, pounding the top of the tower with rain and lashing it with wind. Daphne peered down but could not see the others through the mist. She prayed nothing had happened to them, especially Paul.

Splashing sounded from the left, much heavier than a torrential rain hitting the bay. She cautiously made her way to the end of the tower and looked down the side. Attracted by the noise, the deaders on the opposite bridge had flocked to the guardrail, thousands of them desperate to get at the food. Some reached out too far and fell over the guardrail. Others were shoved over by the horde behind them. Many attempted to jump the gap between the two bridges, an impossible task, sailing and snarling to their watery graves. Good riddance. So many bodies crashed into the bay Daphne could see the froth churning even from this altitude.

Daphne suddenly realized that they were close to a thousand feet above sea level. Dizziness washed over her. She quickly yet cautiously stepped back, careful not to get too close to the tower's edges, then sat down with Akiko and Toshii to wait for the others.

SPARKY REACHED THE top of the tower. He seemed nervous. Walking past Daphne, he sat on the opposite edge near the southern suspension cable.

"Where are the others?"

"Behind me." He avoided making eye contact.

"I thought I heard screaming."

"I didn't hear anything," Sparky snapped and turned his back on Daphne.

AFTER ANOTHER TEN minutes of climbing, Paul spotted the

top of the tower. Daphne sat beside Akiko and Toshii. On seeing him, she jumped up and rushed over, clutching the hand cables as she waited. When he reached the top, she threw her arms around his neck and hugged him tight.

"I'm so glad you made it. I thought I had lost you on the bridge."

"I told you I'd be okay." Paul lovingly rubbed Daphne's back and gently moved her out of the way. "I need to help the others."

Ed reached the tower next, still devastated by the loss of Becca. He refused Paul's help and crossed over to the aviation light stand where he slouched down against it. Next arrived Lisa. Paul gave her credit. She had climbed the main cable in her bare feet, which were bleeding and bruised, and wearing only a red dress soaked with rain. She had not complained once. Taking Lisa's hand, Paul helped her onto the tower and warned her to be careful. She sat by Akiko and checked her bruised feet.

Daphne stared down the main cable. "What happened to Becca."

"She didn't make it." The gruff way he spoke indicated he didn't want to talk about it.

"What now?" asked Lisa.

"We relax for a few minutes then make our way down to safety."

Sparky sat by the southern suspension cable looking down. "You may want to rethink that option."

"Why?" asked Paul as he joined Sparky. "Fuck."

The noise created by saving Lisa and crossing the northern approaches of the span had attracted the attention of those deaders along the southern banks of the bay. Two to three hundred gathered on the bridge at the base of the tower, scratching at the supports in a desperate attempt to get at the food six hundred feet above them.

Chapter Twenty-Four

E D AND DAPHNE joined them. The latter sighed. "We can't catch a fucking break."

"It's just a glitch," Paul reassured her. "We've come this far. The rest will be easy."

Daphne smiled. "You're such an optimist."

"He's such an ass," replied Sparky. "How do you plan on getting past all those things."

"You and I are going to create a diversion while the others escape." He turned to Daphne. "You should go now while it's still pouring. The rain will provide cover."

"What about you?"

"Sparky and I will cover your escape. Once you reach the shore, find a safe place to hide. We'll catch up with you."

"You better." Daphne kissed Paul and then gathered up the rest of the group.

Ed wandered over. "You want me to help?"

"You stay with the others. Sparky and I'll be fine."

"Are you sure?" Ed glared at the kid.

"I'm sure."

"Alright. See you on the other side."

Daphne lined up the others by the southern suspension cable, herself in the lead followed by Toshii, Akiko, Lisa, and Ed. One by one, they climbed off the tower and made their way down.

DAPHNE HATED THIS part worse than the climb. Then, she had focused her attention on the top of the tower, distracting her from how high up they were. Going down, she could not help but notice the bridge six hundred feet below her and the bay another two hundred feet beyond. Panic welled up inside her. Daphne swallowed her fears and kept moving. At least she had become used to walking along the casing, so the trip down went much faster.

Checking on the others, they seemed to be making satisfactory progress, each more confident in their abilities to navigate the suspension cable.

From the top of the tower, yelling and gunfire erupted.

PAUL FIRED DOWN into the horde. At this range, the bullets would have negligible effect other than stinging them with buckshot, but it succeeded in keeping their attention focused on him and Sparky rather than those descending.

Paul interspersed firing a round with banging the stock of his Vepr against the metal floor and taunting, "Come and get us, you motherfuckers."

Sparky's bullets from the hunting rifle were more effective, each shot blowing apart the head of a member of the horde.

Both men kept up the distraction for ten minutes until Sparky checked his pocket. "I'm out of ammo."

"Just keep their attention focused up here for a few more minutes." Paul stepped away from the edge to reload.

Sparky unzipped his fly, freed himself, and released a stream of piss on the deaders. "How are we getting out of here without having those things follow us?"

"I have that covered."

"What's the plan?"

Paul finished reloading the shotgun, stepped up behind Sparky, and shoved him. Sparky toppled over the side, screaming. He landed in the center of the horde. Those not crushed or injured by his body tore into him, ripping off limbs and tearing off chunks of flesh. Fights broke out among the deaders as they struggled to grab the legs and arms from each other. The rest piled onto the corpse, each one that was close enough snatching a piece of skin or organ to feast on.

Staring at the mayhem below, Paul provided the only eulogy of which he could think.

"Looks like you were finally good for something."

Shouldering the Vepr, Paul ran over to the southern suspension cable and began his descent.

DAPHNE AND THE others had closed to within fifty feet of the main span of the bridge. The further they descended, the greater their confidence became. She personally felt a sense of relief when the drop into the bay decreased down to a little over one hundred feet. The fall would still kill her, yet it gave her a weird sense of security.

Once at the bottom, Daphne stopped the others, searching the area for deaders and listening for any danger close by. Between the rain and the commotion from the tower, her visibility and hearing were poor. She felt confident nothing was nearby. Even so, she whistled once, wanting to be certain before descending onto bridge and the exposing the group.

Nothing responded.

Daphne climbed down from the guardrail and shouldered her Mossberg, then reached up for Akiko.

"I'll help you," she whispered.

Akiko positioned herself on the guardrail, her hands clutching the cables for dear life. She released her grip and fell to the side toward the bridge. Daphne helped break her fall and lowered the woman onto asphalt. Toshii needed no help, dismounting like a child getting off a carnival ride. He ran over and hugged his mother. Lisa required assistance getting down because her feet were sore and bloody. The young woman leaned against the guardrail, alternating between raising her legs so to take the pressure off her soles. Ed jumped down last.

"Are you okay?" Daphne asked.

"No," he replied, understanding what she referred to. "I will be after some time."

"I'm sorry. I know—"

A growl came from farther down the bridge toward shore. Akiko gasped and pushed Toshii behind her. Lisa limped away from the guardrail to join Daphne and Ed.

"What is it?"

"I don't know." Ed raised his weapon.

Daphne placed her hand on the barrel and lowered it, then unsheathed her hunting knife. "Let me take it down quietly so we don't attract attention."

Inching forward, Daphne braced herself for the attack, praying it was a single deader and not part of a pack. The footsteps drew closer. Daphne swallowed hard. Her fingers massaged the handle as her mind conjured up every scenario that could play itself out, all of them bad. A figure moved through the shadows, drawing nearer. Daphne prepared to lunge at the deader.

Then it whimpered.

Gojira raced up to Daphne, his stubby tail wagging and his tongue hanging out of his mouth. He rubbed against Daphne's legs, excited to see her. On spotting Toshii, the dog bolted over. Toshii knelt onto the bridge and hugged Gojira tight, receiving a face bath in return.

Lisa was confused. "What's that?"

Toshii beamed. "He's my dog. I named him Gojira."

"I mean, where did he come from?"

Daphne shrugged but was still glad to see him.

"With all the ruckus we created over here, he must have backtracked and crossed the bay on the other bridge," began Ed. "Then he came looking for us."

"I'm glad he did." Toshii ruffled the dog's ear. "Who's a

good boy?"

A minute later, Paul came down and joined them.

Daphne scanned the main cable. "Where's Sparky?"

"He didn't make it." Paul spoke the words with no emotion.

"No loss," Akiko mumbled under her breath.

Ed nodded his understanding.

"Come on," urged Paul. "Let's get off this bridge before that horde of deaders figures out we're here."

Chapter Twenty-Five

PAUL'S GROUP ENCOUNTERED no deaders. Those on both bridges were attracted to the center and still searching for the food that had since departed. A handful shambled around where the span connected to the mainland, oblivious to them, the rain providing cover. Circling around under the twin bridges, they made their way along shore away from Annapolis.

Half a mile down the coast, they stumbled across a three-story mansion a dozen yards inland. Paul led them around to the front. Nothing moved in the area and no lights shone from inside. Suitcases and travel bags sat in the driveway, indicating the occupants had left in a hurry. Climbing the stairs onto the front porch, Paul checked the front door. No one had locked it.

Paul pushed open the door and raised his Vepr. "Is anyone here?"

Nothing responded, either living or living dead.

"We're coming in. We're only looking for a place to rest."

Silence.

Paul ushered everyone inside, closing and locking the door behind him.

"You stay here while Daphne and I check it out."

The two conducted a room-by-room search but found nothing unusual except piles of clothes on the floor in each of the bedrooms and canned food spread out across the kitchen counter. They rejoined the others.

"The place is clear. There's food in the kitchen so feel free to help yourselves. Just stay quiet and don't turn on any lights. We don't want to draw attention."

As Paul and Ed moved the sofa, lodging it between the front door and the stairwell so nothing could break in, Akiko and Toshii headed to the kitchen. Gojira followed, hoping for something to eat. Daphne and Lisa raided the upstairs linen closet, bringing back a bunch of towels that everyone used to dry off. Lisa returned upstairs and soon came down dressed in jeans, a white shirt, and sneakers. She joined them in the kitchen where everyone stood around the island eating cold food out of cans.

Paul finished off his fruit salad. "We'll stay here tonight, rest up and dry off, and plan our next course of action in the morning."

"Will we be safe?" asked Akiko.

"We should be for the night. Everyone, fill your backpacks with as much food as you can carry and then grab a bedroom upstairs and get some sleep. Keep your weapons and backpacks nearby and be ready to move quickly if necessary. I'll keep watch."

"You need sleep, too," protested Daphne.

"What time is it?"

Lisa checked her watch. "A little before one."

"We'll switch out at 0400. Does that sound good?"

Daphne nodded.

"Everyone rest up. You'll need it for tomorrow."

One by one, the others filtered upstairs, Daphne being the last to leave.

"Are you sure you don't want me to stay down here with you?"

"I'll be fine. Get some rest and replace me in three hours."

"You got it." Daphne kissed him and headed to the bedrooms.

Paul made his way to the love seat in front of the fireplace and sat down. He considered stripping out of his wet clothes but thought better about it, not wanting to be caught naked if the shit hit the fan. Instead, he removed a knit comforter from the armrest and wrapped it around him, then sat down with the Vepr in his lap.

The events of the last forty-eight hours flooded his mind, a blur of unpleasant memories. It was amazing that they had survived so long. Well, not everyone. Considering what they had gone through, though, the fact that any of them had made it this far was a miracle.

Paul tried to console himself with the thought that things could only get better, then quickly erased that misconstrued concept. He knew it wouldn't. Society had fallen apart overnight. By this time tomorrow, everyone would be fending for themselves. The government. The Police. The military. And those fortunate enough to have survived the outbreak. For every decent person like Ed, he reasoned there were a dozen Sparky types out there. From here on in, his group would be facing a struggle for survival between humans and the dead. The prospects for the future were not promising.

As his thoughts turned to Alissa and how she had fared during the apocalypse, Paul fell asleep.

A Preview of *Operation Majestic*

(To be released in December 2021)

Summary: Think *Raiders of the Lost Ark* meets *Back to the Future* – with aliens.

Cairo, Egypt
Present day

A N INTENSE MID-DAY sun blared down on the desert, reflecting off the sand so brightly that not even the Rayban sunglasses Pierre wore could lessen all the glare. The shimmering heat emanating from the desert distorted the Pyramids of Giza two miles to the north, rendering their image on the horizon like that of a mirage. Even within the shades of his tent the temperature topped one hundred. As soon as Pierre swiped a cloth across his forehead, more beads of sweat formed and ran down into his eyes, stinging them. He did not let the heat and discomfort bother him. A few minor hardships were a small price to pay. Pierre was on the brink of making one of the most significant discoveries in Egyptian archaeology since the discovery of King Tut's tomb a century ago.

Pierre stood at the entrance to his tent, watching as his crew, several dozen local excavators supervised by two of his graduate students from Cambridge University, dug up the surrounding fifty acres. The area had been discovered a year and a half ago when a ground penetrating radar mapping the desert surrounding the pyramids detected an anomaly the size of a small town two miles southeast of the pyramids. That was the easy part. It required a year of negotiating with the new director of Minister of State for Antiquities, a man who did little to conceal his anti-Western bias, before the Egyptian government granted permission for Pierre to excavate the site under the stipulation that all artifacts belonged to the museum, a condition that suited Pierre. He was more interested in having his name associated with the discovery than with the potential wealth.

So far, the artifacts unearthed had been neither numerous or extraordinary: a discarded sack of pottery that probably fell off a trading caravan; an abandoned campsite; and sundry other objects. What fascinated Pierre, however, was that the depth of each discovery corelated to an era further in the past, indicating they were excavating a pristine location, one not seen by human eyes in millennium. His expectations were confirmed nine weeks ago when his team uncovered the wall of an intact building. Since then, his team had uncovered four buildings, each one composed of the same material used to construct the worker compound near the Pyramids, confirming that the structures were four thousand fiver hundred years old, the same age as the Pyramid of Khufu. Unlike the ones at the workers compound, these were constructed in a slightly different style, implying they may have had a different purpose. With luck, his team would make a new discovery that would earn them a place in archaeological history.

"A watched pot never boils." The voice came from Hans Erntsmann, the senior Cairo correspondent for *National Geographic*, who sat in front of Pierre's desk. The German had been following Pierre's dig since the discovery began six months ago. A seasoned journalist and one of the best in his field, an article by Ernstmann would ensure one's place in archaeological history. Ernstmann's standing allowed him to give play to his eccentricity. The journalist wore an outfit that reminded Pierre of the American's conception of an archaeologist from the 1930s: ankle-high boots with shin-high wool socks, tan shorts with exterior pockets, and a matching short-sleeve shirt with epaulettes. Pierre found the quirkiness endearing.

"I can't help it." Pierre stepped back inside the tent.

"Don't you trust Janet and Seth?"

"It's Janice." Pierre opened the cooler and removed a plastic bottle from the ice. "And yes, I have full confidence in them. They're the best grad students I've ever worked with."

"Then what's the problem?"

Pierre sat down behind his desk and opened the bottle. "The problem is I'm stuck in here when I want to be out there involved in the dig."

"We have to pass the torch to the next generation at some time."

"I don't see you stepping aside," chuckled Pierre as he swigged a mouthful of cold water.

"Don't let my charming presence fool you," teased Hans. "My editor sent the new correspondent to Korea to write about how wildlife has flourished in the Demilitarized Zone since the end of the Korean War. They're talking about turning it into a TV special. I'm here because I got the pick of the sloppy seconds, and because I like you."

Pierre laughed. "I'm touched."

"You should be." Hans raised his bottle of water in a mock toast.

"I'm just afraid this will be my last dig."

"University pressuring you to spend more time lecturing?"

"Yeah." Pierre frowned. "Don't get me wrong. I love teaching. But fieldwork is my passion."

"At least you'll end your time in the field on a high note."

"What do you mean?"

"You're about to make one of the biggest archaeological discoveries in the past two hundred years."

"Do you really think so?"

"Of course. Your team has uncovered a village that has been buried for five millennia. No matter what you find, it'll rank up there with the discovery of the tombs of the pyramid builders and the unearthing of the Sphinx, and your name will be associated with it."

Pierre smiled. "I hope you're right."

"Of course, I am. I've been in this business—" A commotion broke out at the dig site, with the workers yelling in Arabic. A moment later, someone ran toward the tent. Hans pointed toward the approaching footsteps. "See, you're about to go down in history."

The supervisor of the Egyptian workers burst into the tent. His panting to catch his breath mixed with excitement made it more difficult than usual to understand him. "Come quick. You needed at site."

"Where's Janice?"

"She sent me." The supervisor retreated several feet and waved for Pierre to join him. "Hurry. Come quick. You needed. Please, hurry."

Pierre jumped up and raced after the supervisor, followed by Hans. The three wound their way through the excavation site to where a group of workers stood around the rim of a dig. He knew by the fear and anxiety on their faces that whatever caused the uproar was not good. As the Europeans reached the edge of the dig, the workers moved aside, allowing them access. Janice stood up the bottom, taking photos with her cell phone. Her usually calm manner seemed rattled. The supervisor caught Pierre's attention and pointed to the building they had unearthed.

"See. See."

Pierre glanced over to the structure. A section of the upper wall had been exposed above the top of what appeared to be an entranceway. His attention focused on the symbol above the door. Pierre was speechless.

Hans mumbled, "*Mein verdammter Gott.*"

Descending the slope of the dig, Pierre crossed over to the symbol and ran his fingertips across its surface. "This can't be real?"

"It is," Janice replied. "It has the same weathering pattern as the rest of the wall. As best as I can tell from a visual examination, it's at least four thousand years old."

Pierre stared at the symbol, shocked by the implications. His name would be associated with this discovery, but not in the way he had hoped. Removing his cell phone from his back pocket, Pierre took photographs of the symbol, wondering how he would explain this to the university.

A Thank You to My Readers

In addition to working for the CIA and being a stepdad, writing has been one of the most fulfilling things I've done with my life. The best part is having fans who read my books, enjoy them, and crave more. I'm incredibly fortunate and grateful I have such a loyal fanbase. You keep reading, and I'll keep writing.

If you enjoyed *The Chronicles of Paul*, please post a review on Amazon and Goodreads. Reviews are what drive the algorithms that get a writer's books more exposure. It doesn't have to be lengthy—just a rating and a sentence or two about why you liked it. To be successful, I need your support.

A final note. The *Nurse Alissa vs. the Zombies* series will continue as will the Tatyana paranormal stories. I'm currently writing *Nurse Alissa vs. the Zombies VIII* and am in the process of plotting out the next Tatyana novel (which will take place aboard a haunted cruise ship) and the next book in *The Chronicles of Paul* saga.

Thank you all in advance.

Acknowledgments

The fun part of my job is writing. The difficult part is getting my books published. It's a complicated process involving many people, all of whom deserve to be recognized.

I want to thank my social media manager for urging me to write a spin-off of *Nurse Alissa vs. the Zombies*. As you can tell, *The Chronicles of Paul* has a more action-packed, *Dead Rising* feel about it. I meant it to be that way. Paul, Daphne, and the gang who I decide not to kill of will be around for a while. While I still plan to keep the plots realistic (or as realistic as a zombie apocalypse can be), I intend to incorporate some impressive zombie kills that Alissa can't do now that she's in the desert.

Many thanks also go out to my beta readers, most of whom have been with me from book one. They point out grammatical/spelling errors and inconsistencies and offer their opinion on whether they like the story. I would be lost without them. This book, as all my others, is a much better read because of them.

Christian Bentulan, who already does the cover designs for the *Nurse Alissa* series, did the cover art for *The Chronicles of Paul*. His work perfectly fits the mood of this book. I'm looking forward to collaborating with him.

Finally, a major debt of thanks goes to my family, human and furry. Working from home allows me to set my hours, though it's rare if I work less than ten hours a day. The pets are always there as my muses and distractions. Walther and Bella sit with me on my porch while I write during the day (except in the freezing weather when they abandon me for a warm bed) and, at night, when I'm in my study editing and managing social media, my cats Archer and Michonne stand in front of my desktop computer, Michonne because she wants to be petted and Archer to meow because he ran of treats or because he can see the bottom of his food dish. My family never complains (I think they're glad to get rid of me). I couldn't do this without their love, patience, and support. I love them all.

About the Author

Scott M. Baker was born and raised in Everett, Massachusetts and spent twenty-three years in northern Virginia working for the Central Intelligence Agency and traveling through Europe, Asia, and the Middle East. Scott is now retired and lives outside of Concord, New Hampshire, with his wife and fellow writer Alison Beightol, his stepdaughter, two rambunctious Boxers, and two cats who treat him as their human servant. He is currently writing the *Nurse Alissa vs. the Zombies* and *The Chronicles of Paul* sagas, his latest zombie apocalypse series, as well as his paranormal series. Previous works include *Frozen World*, his first non-zombie post-apocalypse novel; the *Shattered World* series, his five-book young adult post-apocalypse thriller about a group of adventurers attempting to close interdimensional portals from Hell; *The Vampire Hunters* trilogy, about humans fighting the undead in Washington D.C.; *Rotter World, Rotter Nation,* and *Rotter Apocalypse*, his first post-apocalyptic zombie saga; *Yeitso*, his homage to the giant monster movies of the 1950s that he loved watching as a kid; as well as several zombie-themed novellas and anthologies.

Please check out Scott's social media accounts for the latest information on future books, upcoming events, and other fun stuff.

Facebook: facebook.com/groups/397749347486177
Twitter: twitter.com/vampire_hunters
Instagram: instagram.com/scottmbakerwriter
Blog: scottmbakerauthor.blogspot.com

You can also sign up for Scott's newsletter which will be released on the 1st and 15th of every month. He promises not to share your email with anyone or spam the recipients. The newsletter will contain advance notices of upcoming releases/events and will soon contain short stories from the Alissa, Paul, and Tatyana universes that will not be available to the public. You can sign up by clicking the link below.

Newsletter: mailchi.mp/0b1401f1ddb2/scott-m-baker-writer